NEVER LESS

WE ALL NEED A SAFETY NET, BUT NEED A TRUE FRIEND
EVEN MORE...

THE PABLO AND MINDY MYSTERIES
BOOK ONE

GEOFFREY WELLS

YOU'RE INVITED

Hello.

Before you get started, I want you to know, at the back of the book you're invited to join my Readers Group so that you can keep updated on my new releases and other writerly things.

And please note, if you need them, or someone you know needs them, there are addiction resources at the back of the book.

Take care of each other and thank you for spending your time reading my story.

Geoffrey.

~

Walking with a friend in the dark is better than walking alone in the light.
~*Helen Keller*

The only way to have a friend is to be one.
~*Ralph Waldo Emerson*

~

PROLOGUE

Hi. I'm Mindy. Let's understand each other before I get started—this story is about me.

This story is not about Pablo, just so we're clear. It's not a story about what people think of Pablo, what he's not doing right, or if he's smart or stupid, good or bad. Or too short. 'Cause I couldn't tell you. Maybe he's all of those things. Sometimes he makes me think I'm the dumb one. Or too tall.

So, if you're thinking I'm going to tell you there's something wrong with him because he makes his own rules, or his easy way with people makes him a pushover, then I promise you—you'll have to rethink that idea.

I'm still trying to figure him out myself. But let me start then. You'll see; I have an odd friend.

You'll get over it.

HOW I MET MINDY

PABLO

I MET MINDY THREE YEARS AGO ON THE FIRST DAY OF THE SCHOOL year. I was new, and I was late.

When Dad dropped me off at the curb, he told me it was a good school. He would have liked to have gone to it. "You'll learn to be an American here," he said in Spanish. "So, make the best of it. I know you'll do well."

"Thanks, Dad," I said.

A new school again. I'd had a year in San Diego, then two years at that school in Fresno. I was losing count, but I would never forget this one, though I didn't know that at the time.

It was my first school outside of California and I knew nothing about the East Coast or Long Island. I did know I was in for a long day. I checked in my backpack for my wrapped lunch that Mom had made, and I had a good pen—I was prepared. Besides, our family was tough. I'd be okay.

It seemed weird that I couldn't blend in with the other kids when I arrived. There were none around. A lady took my hand, which I yanked back into my shorts pocket. She knew my name and led me past empty schoolrooms with walls covered by large maps, good-work badges and good-student names. My stomach churned as I wondered if I'd be good enough.

As we approached the library, I heard the murmuring voices of kids. The lady led me around the little kids seated cross legged on the carpeted floor, to a noisy crowd of boys my age at the back who all looked like experienced middle school guys. They parted as the lady ushered me forward into the group. They frowned at her and then at me.

I smiled at them, as a way of saying sorry for breaking up their fun and laughter.

"Hey, you guys," she said, "say hi to your new classmate, Pablo."

She patted my shoulder and walked away.

I shook my head and smiled. I wanted to say, *hola*, but couldn't think of the word they would use. It wasn't hello.

As the principal started his welcome speech, someone bumped me. It was almost a shove; maybe they wanted to get by. But I felt pulling on the waistband of my shorts. He wasn't pulling me aside; he was pulling them down. Tugging my shorts down. Then, from behind, someone's running shoe hooked into the waistband of my shorts and stomped them to the floor.

With my arms hanging at my sides, I dropped my chin into my chest and looked down at my shorts over my ankles, at my white briefs, my bare shins sprouting out of them—and couldn't move. The boys snickered and I cowered. My hands shook and I felt like my knees would fold under me and I'd collapse trembling at their feet. I couldn't even scowl back at them. My cheeks burned, and the tingling in my face made my hearing dull except for a high-pitched whine.

I yanked up my shorts and pretended to listen to the principal with my thumbs firmly hooked into my waistband in case they tried it again. The principal's eyes stopped on me for a split second and then he continued with his message of wanting everyone to win at his school. I didn't know where to look. This didn't feel like winning.

I didn't understand what had happened, but I was certain *why* it had happened—I was the new kid, the late boy, the Mexican boy, the outsider who didn't look like them, who didn't speak English good, who was short and whose dark skin stood out in the sea of white faces. I was a loser to them.

After the speech, the public address system blared something I didn't quite get. But everyone else got it. I shuffled out with them, not knowing where I was going. I just moved with them and hoped I didn't end up in the wrong place. How foolish I would feel—all over again. The boys ahead of me were buddies, excited to be together. They'd probably been classmates for years, so breaking through and making friends was not going to happen.

I would keep my mouth shut and make the best of it, as Dad said I should. He could never know about this—and would be furious if he found out. He would never understand how much I wanted to be like the American kids. He wanted me to prove to him that the Cruz family life here in the US did not have to be one disaster after the next.

I wouldn't tell Mom either. She'd tell me to get over it. Suck it up. That's what I would have to do.

Long after that happened, as I moved through the hallways, I felt their eyes on my bare parts. Looking at me, judging me. I still could not make eye contact, but I heard the loud boy. I looked behind me. He smirked and looked away. He was brave enough in front of his friends to pull my shorts down, but not brave enough to insult me to my face. Yet, if I accused him it would turn into a fight, which I would lose. The truth was I was both too proud and too ashamed—if that's possible—of my own stupidity.

How could I have let that happen to me?

∿

MY MEMORY OF THAT MORNING AFTER THEY DID THAT TO ME WAS of classrooms and teachers and me trying to understand what everything meant. Most the time I wasn't sure what the subjects were, except for math.

As that class let out, a girl asked, "What's your name?" She was quite a bit taller than me, skinny with blue eyes and skinny pale hair and skin.

She shot out her hand. "I'm Melinda."

I hoped so hard that she hadn't seen me earlier, but then I realized she would never have talked to me if she had seen me with my shorts around my ankles. She'd find out, for sure though, so I had better make the best of it while I could.

"I'm Pablo," I said and shook her hand. "Pablo Cruz."

"Cool name. They call me Mindy."

I wanted to say how nice it was to talk to her—that she had no idea how wonderful it was for me to be seen and spoken to.

Instead, I said what Mom taught me to say: It's a pleasure to meet you, then I added, "Thank you."

"For what?" she asked.

I smiled and said the first thing that came into my head. "For being you."

Her face lit up with a petty smile. "Oh? No prob, Pablo. Anytime."

Mindy gave me hope. I felt like she was restarting my life, turning my whole world from miserable into something exciting and fun. After that, all I'd have to do was remember we were friends, and that I would keep the promise I'd just made to myself: I would do anything for Mindy and I would never, ever tell her what happened in the library. She would have to find out for herself.

But maybe she wouldn't.

2

THREE YEARS LATER

MINDY

PABLO WAS NOT AT SCHOOL TODAY, BUT HE MET ME ON THE SOCCER field later in the afternoon. He came from working with his dad, chopping down trees.

We've been practicing passing the ball for the past hour. He expects to have it perfectly returned to him every time. I watch how effortlessly he does it. But when I pass it back my aim is off and the ball skids to the side. No problem for him of course; he's on it in a second. He's a stocky guy and can pounce as quick as a cat. He flips the ball up with his foot, taps it onto his other boot—bounce, bounce—then grounds it to a dead stop. A quick cutback and a tap with the back of his foot rolls the ball behind him. He spins and kicks, as if in slow motion—*thwat*! He nails the return right back at me.

"Like that," he says.

Nice. I have a lot to learn.

"You do it," he calls out to me, "Like in a FIFA match."

"What's a fever match?" I ask.

"Not fever, *fiver*," he says slowly, or that's what it sounds like to me.

So, I stop and google it on my phone. He comes over and scans the search results with me. "There," he says. "FIFA Club World Cup football. But it's not football; it's soccer—big time. For the best teams in the world. But Mindy, sorry, gotta go now."

"Already? We've only been here an hour. Now suddenly you have to go? I never know where your head is," I say. "What's going on?"

He looks down, fidgeting. I'm pretty certain he's not leaving because of me. My theory is his homework is not done. He'll get into trouble again. Unfortunately, his schoolwork is far from perfect, although he is the best in art class. Miss Lopez, our math teacher calls him a dreamer, though I think she means Dreamer, 'cause she says it like she knows all about it. It annoys Pablo to no end because she can't know what it's like. Nor do I, but it doesn't matter—he treats me like I'm one of the guys on his soccer team, and I love it. He doesn't care that I'm a girl.

"Mindy, could you help me with something?"

"Maybe. What is it?"

"I dropped my pocketknife and can't find it. I could use another pair of eyes."

Even though we practice longer on Friday afternoons, it is getting late. But this must be important to him because he's admitting to me that he can't do this by himself.

"Now?" I ask. "Why couldn't you just pick it up?"

"I was forty feet up a tree, trimming a branch. When it fell, it knocked my pocketknife out of my hand. The platform was swaying so much I couldn't watch it fall because I had to hold on with both hands."

"So that's why you weren't at school today? Why didn't you stay to look for it while it was still light?" I ask.

He rests his foot on the soccer ball. "My dad gave it to me for

9

my birthday. I couldn't tell him. It's like I threw my present away," he says.

"Oh." Now I get it. "But you didn't throw it away, did you?"

"Well . . . that's how it looks," he says and picks up the ball with his hands—which looks weird.

"I should go home," I say. "So should you."

He steps away and drops the ball onto his foot. He bounces it onto the other foot, then back again, like he's juggling. He's pretending he didn't hear me—he does that. He heard what I said, but he's not taking no for an answer. I stare at him to make sure he's for real, but there are no secrets with Pablo. This is just his way of waiting for me to come around and agree to his request.

It's getting late. And here I am, seriously considering helping him look for his knife—just the two of us, in the forest, in the dark, almost. It doesn't make sense but I don't care—many things in my life don't make sense.

Like, the reason I'm here is to get away, to leave the noises at our house—the creaking walls, the tapping water pipes, and the hum of the fridge. These sounds are not scary because I know what they are—and because I'm twelve. But they bring me down. I have to listen to them because Dad might need me. After homework I should be doing other things like texting friends, or whatever. But that doesn't help. I hear the noises because I'm always listening for Dad, even though I know he's asleep upstairs. So, I pick up the nagging silence in the house when he's taken his meds.

What worries me is his breathing. Ever since that delivery van t-boned his car on Route 48, I've been listening. Of course, he feels no pain from the pills.

Of course, none of that matters here on the soccer field with these friendly sounds—the cleat on summer grass, the wind rattling the oak leaves in the trees surrounding the field, the thwack of the ball as Pablo kicks it back.

These last few September afternoons the sun has been setting a little earlier and it no longer takes forever to go from dark to black. All I want to do is forget and focus on getting control of that ball. I don't have this much trouble with my classwork, or anything else —I make sure of that. But soccer and the soundless noise at home make me feel like a failure.

"Let's go find your knife," I say.

It's late now, and I think I hear an owl.

WE'VE WALKED UP THE STEEP ROAD TO THE TOP OF THE RIDGE that overlooks the Long Island Sound. Pablo takes a driveway through the trees. "It's this way," he says.

The horizon sky above the sound has turned green, signaling the last light of the day. We've come to a collapsed chain-link fence. On the other side are the freshly cut branches. Rubble fills in a dip in the ground that was once quite deep. Some distance away, a dark house lurks behind trees. We step over the fencing and stare into the pit.

"Okay, so it fell into this pile of branches," he says, shaking his head. "We might not find it."

No kidding. But I'm not going to stand around thinking about what we might not find. "Well, we won't know until we try," I say.

He nods and begins to root through the thicket of fallen branches.

The pit is a mess. There's an old lawnmower from way back when people still pushed those things around, and a sorry-looking dishwasher with its door gaping open like it died from COVID. And over there, pieces of an old shack have fallen in. A beam sticks out on one side. In the half-light, I see it has a rusted bolt connecting it to another beam and maybe there's another one further in the side of the hole.

I root around in the thicket surrounding the pit thinking the knife might not have fallen in. Meanwhile, Pablo is turning things over, crouching to peer between the junk, using his phone's flashlight.

"We're not going to find it in the dark," I call out to him. "Let's come back in the morning." What we might find is something we don't want to see.

Did his dad even care? It's weird that they stayed that late trimming trees—especially when his son should have been at school. "So, this is why you weren't at school?" I ask.

"My dad needed me. His workers have COVID."

And yet, he still came to practice drills with me. That's how certain he is I could be a good soccer player. But now I have to stop him because he won't stop searching.

I give him a quick wave. "I'm leaving, Pablo."

He looks up. "I'm coming."

From what I can see, finding Pablo's present isn't going to make him feel better. It won't help his family's legal status. It won't save his dad's tree business if his dad gets arrested. It won't stop the bus that ships him back to Mexico. Whether found or lost, the knife is not going to make Pablo a better student. Watching him down there in the pit I wonder how I would do in school if I were him; would I get the answers right if I didn't fully understand the questions?

We walk back to the soccer field, not saying much. "I know

leaving your knife somewhere in the hole is horrible for you, but we'll come back early tomorrow morning. Okay?"

He nods, his lips pressed together in a thin line.

3

THE BEDROOM

WHEN I GET HOME AFTER THAT STUPID SEARCH AT THE HOLE, THE house is quiet. Everything is in order. Mom has spread a rustic fall runner on the dining room table. I hear the refrigerator making ice as I pause to take off my shoes to carry them across the thick pile carpet into the kitchen.

On the kitchen counter I find a note from Mom saying to call her ASAP. I check my phone—oh, shucks, I missed her text. She's at the soccer field trying to find me. But where is Dad? I'll quickly check on Dad before I call her back.

His car is in the garage. I go upstairs and call softly, not wanting to wake him.

Nothing.

I step lightly into their bedroom at the end of the hallway. The door is slightly ajar. "Dad?" I say, a little louder.

I push the door open. He's sleeping with the bedcover over his head. I stare, my eyes glued to the rise and fall of his shallow breathing. Then I hear that small moan, like a baby—a muffled sob that doesn't sound like Dad. There's a slight movement of the covers.

I come closer. "Dad?"

He throws the bed cover off and swivels around to look at me with frightened eyes so wide I see why they call them eyeballs. He's still in his suit, but his tie has twisted around and his shirt is wet from sweat. His arm has come out of his sling, which is now wrapped around his neck like a scarf.

"M'ndy," he slurs.

"Dad, are you all right?"

He tries to raise himself onto his elbows, then remembers his arm is broken and flops back. "I'm not well, Mindy," he says. With eyes shut tight he says, "I need help."

"What can I do? Should I call 911?"

His eyes roll back. "No, no. *Please do not do that.* Oh. God. Help me," he whimpers.

I want to hug him but I can't bring myself to get closer. He smells of aftershave mixed with that dog smell of icky sweat. This is not my father. I'm looking at a suffering stranger. A ghost of the man who's still in pain and who has lost control. He falls back onto the pillow and is instantly asleep.

I look around the amazingly neat bedroom. There is nothing on Mom's or Dad's bedside table. The closet doors are closed. There's nothing on the floor, not even a sock near the bed. There's nothing interesting here, so how does he get into this state of pain? I can only guess it's from his crushed shoulder after his accident. Or is this crazed state caused by the painkillers he takes?

The bathroom is just as neat. I look small reflected in the double mirror over the vanity. The medicine chest door clicks open when I push it in. There is the razor and next to it a fancy bottle of what looks like Mom's perfume. The label says it's aftershave. With the top off, it's so strong I hold it away with my arm outstretched. I screw the top on tightly. I place it back on his shelf between the razor and a tubular pill, one half light brown, the other green. I reach for it and bump the pill. It rolls off the glass shelf, falls into the sink, and circles the drain hole. I grab it before it disappears. When I open my hand, I see I have crushed the pill—the capsule has split open, but there's still powder left in one half.

"Ah, jees," I mutter. He'll need the pill, but I can't put it back broken. My heart is racing. Is this pill what he takes to get him through the night? Because where's the bottle? Important pills come in bottles with complicated labels, which I can google, but not now. So, I slip the pill into my jeans pocket and softly close the medicine chest.

Tiptoeing out of the bedroom I hear Mom below. I go down and meet her in the kitchen.

"You never called me," Mom says, flinging her handbag onto the counter.

"Sorry, Mom. I wanted to check on Dad."

Mom ignores me as she unloads the dishwasher, stacks dinner plates, makes loud clattering sounds. Then she stops to look at me for the first time. "And? How is he? He was asleep when I left you the note."

"Yup. Not a peep from him," I say.

"So…no big theory from Doctor MacKay today?"

"Nope. Not even a, 'hear's the thing' story. But here *is* the thing, Mom, I think there's something seriously wrong with Dad."

I watch her face as she watches me. There's no change. Like usual she's got her own ideas about what's going on and whatever I'm thinking she's not taking it seriously.

"It's the pain. That's what makes him crazy," Mom says. She always says this about Dad. "He'll sleep it off."

I can't tell Mom about the pill—if she asks. She'll see him in a few minutes and draw her own conclusions. But what will they think when he tells her to get him the pill that is now in my pocket?

Then the questions will come. Endless questions.

Should I tell her the truth? I wanted to see why he smelled so bad, why he was in so much pain when *he's* the doctor, but I can't say that.

So, I'm going to say nothing—which, I know, is like a lie. And the best way to get away with it is to show them that I do my homework when I get home. But they know that because I get good grades. I don't poke around in his things. I don't lie—much. That's not me. I am a good girl.

Really.

4

PETER AND CANDY

MINDY

EARLY ON THIS MILD SATURDAY MORNING PABLO AND I HAVE returned to look for his knife at the hole. To get to the driveway we walk fast up the country road that slopes gently past the sunflower field, then rises more steeply to the crest. Last night I'd seen the big house, its blackness sinking into the forest. But at the edge of the bluff, I also remember seeing a killer view of Long Island Sound and the inlet below.

We hardly notice an old man walking his old dog down the slope toward us on the other side of the road. We pass him as if he wasn't there. I'm sure he thinks nothing of a couple of kids walking up the road. Maybe he thinks we're brother and sister—maybe not on second thought—but when we turn up the driveway he calls out after us.

"Hey, guys. You know, that's not a road."

Pablo of course clams up, leaving me frowning at the old man.

I wonder why he cares about us. I know we really shouldn't be going up the drive—it is trespassing. If we'd gone through the forest, we wouldn't have been noticed, but Pablo worries about ticks. Never mind the dangerous work he does; he's obsessed about getting bitten because his family has to pay for medical bills. So, we took the driveway, and now we've been caught, which can't be good.

So, I lie and shout back, "We thought it was a shortcut."

The old man beckons us over. I thought I recognized him. Mom and I bought sunflowers at his farm stand last year. It was Dad's birthday.

We traipse down the drive to talk to him. His dog sits, wagging her tail so fast it might fly off.

"I'm Peter, by the way. Peter King," he says.

I can't resist. "Can I pat your dog?"

"Sure. Candy, say hello," he says.

Meanwhile, Pablo is fidgeting, looking for an escape. *No good can come from this little meeting*, he's probably thinking. Maybe he thinks the dog will snap.

"How old is she?" I ask, stroking Candy's head, as she randomly flings drool from the side of her panting mouth.

Peter smiles and winks at Pablo. "She's twelve. Four years older than me in dog years."

Pablo gives me a blank look and shakes his head.

"Candy is twelve times seven in dog years, which is eighty-four, so Peter is eighty," I quietly explain to Pablo.

"Smart girl," Peter says. "But you were saying: shortcut to where?"

"The top," I say, pointing to the crest of the rise.

"Why?"

"To see the sea...for geography class."

The way Peter looks at me I can see he's not buying my story. "Ah. The sound, you mean." He raises his index finger into the breeze coming over the crest. "So, on a day like this—and I know this because I walk Candy up there every day—I read the weather

19

coming in from Connecticut over the sound," he says. "I look out from the same point every time at a telephone pole, which Candy finds fascinating to pee on. From there, if you look about a mile out over the sound and see the water ruffled by a zephyr, you can bet the weather will be on you within the hour."

"What's a zephyr?" I ask.

"A breeze. A light wind. You can use that for your geography class. However, in your writing class, tell your English teacher it more accurately means a light wind, *coming from the West*."

I love this cool little factoid—just my thing to pull out in English. Now it's my turn to get the wink. He's a winker.

"Well, have a good walk," Peter says. "Candy and I need our kibble, and hey, on the way back give me a wave. I'm the house just after the sunflowers."

5

THE ZEPHYR

PABLO

WE LEAVE PETER AND DECIDE TO TAKE HIS ADVICE . . . SORT OF. Mindy and I don't walk up the driveway, but we do walk up the road to the top of the ridge with the idea of cutting across from there to the hole—to find my knife.

As we come over the crest our eyes drink in the azure sound glistening all the way to the Connecticut shore. We stop to catch our breath as we marvel at the sight. Closer to the Long Island shore below us we see the inlet snaking through the wetland coming out at the marina in the distance.

As I expect, Mindy points out a rough patch far out on the water.

I shake my head. "No, it's not a zephyr."

"How do you know?"

"Because, look," I point. "See, the gulls and terns diving? The fish are ruffling the water. And Mindy, why did you tell him that stuff about geography class?"

"Just . . . Because . . ." Mindy fidgets, and looks out over the sound and avoids my eyes. "I mean, I didn't want to get so deep in the weeds—as my dad says—so I made up a story."

"Yeah, and you got *into* the weeds, even worse. Now you have to remember your excuses—the shortcut excuse and the geography class excuse, and now *I'll* have to remember that zephyrs come from the west."

"Yes, you do. But I didn't want to tell him where we're going. Jeez."

I wave my finger. "God will punish you for that. I'll pray for you tomorrow at mass."

"Right, that's sweet. Please do," she says. "Except, I don't believe you for a second. That's why you go to mass? To pray?"

"Well...we go to St. James Roman Catholic Church because of Sister Loraine Ignacio. She's a DACA activist."

"Remind me. What's that stand for?"

"Deferred Action for Childhood Arrivals, and it's why I can stay in the US—as long as I don't get arrested."

Mindy looks at her watch. "Hey, we need to hustle. My mom's picking me up at my house at nine."

She's right. We're running out of time. I got up early so I would have enough time to come here, look for my knife, and still be at the soccer field by nine for a Saturday game in the rouge league.

We head for the tall copse of trees on the ridge. Below, at the bottom of the bluff boats come and go along the inlet. They're mostly fishing boats out for the early catch. Dad would love to own one of those boats, like the one moored next to the parking lot, behind a large passenger boat running summer day trips. At the end of a ragtag line of shacks along the bank is derelict old mill, and on the other side is a boat warehouse.

The mill looks beyond repair; however, three dudes are tying up a fishing skiff alongside the deck attached to the mill. One of them carrying what appears to be a fishing tackle box and enters the mill through a side door.

"What's happening down there," Mindy asks.

I put my finger over my lips and scowl at her. "I'm trying to hear those guys at the skiff," I say keeping my voice low.

My suspicion is confirmed when I hear occasional snippets of lowlife Spanish floating up the bluff. They must be avoided.

"What's going on?" she asks again.

Across the narrow service road leading into the parking lot is a squat lighthouse-shaped tower. To my surprise, we see the same man exit who'd entered the mill across the street a minute ago.

"How did he get there?" she whispers.

"*El túnel*," I mumble to myself.

"What's that?" Mindy asks, then she's thumb typing on her phone. "I'm getting tulips, the elf tune, and piano tuners . . . hold on . . . ah shucks, that's Mom's text reminding me."

"It's eight oh five," I say. "Let's go. I want to find my pocketknife."

We head for the copse of trees. Mindy follows—not that she has an option—and she's bellyaching all the way.

"They call you a Dreamer, but they should call you a daydreamer," she's muttering.

"They call me that too," I say.

"That's not a compliment, Pablo. It means you're not practical. You're never going to find your knife in that mess, and in the meantime, we're trespassing!"

We move quickly and come to the chain-link fence surrounding the hole. From the other side of the hole, we see a truck approaching on the driveway we'd just walked up.

"Get down," I say, as the truck pulls up next to the hole.

An older man—kind of well-dressed in new Levi's and cowboy

boots—gets out and yanks on work gloves. He walks over to the hole, pauses, pulls out a phone, and grunts into it.

Mindy elbows my ribs and jabs at her own phone, her eyes wide. She's going to be late; I know. So am I. But we can't move.

The man finishes his call. With the winch hook from his front fender, he walks into the pit and then uses his wireless winch remote control to retrieve something.

"It's the same tackle box," Mindy whispers.

The man jerks his head up. He's heard her.

"Hey," he calls out.

We scramble through the thorny underbrush toward the ridge road we'd walked up. The man comes after us, still carrying the red box, but then changes his mind and runs back to his truck. I lead us through the bramble underbrush, lousy with ticks and thorns, and soon we're running down the road, past the steep driveway. As we run past the sunflower field the truck lunges out onto the road. The screaming gear changes are deafening as he accelerates to catch up to us.

"The sunflowers," I shout.

"No. Let's go to Peter's house," Mindy pants.

We dash up Peter's drive and hide behind his boat on its trailer hooked up to his red truck. The man with the tackle box slows to an idle as he cruises past the driveway, then he suddenly roars off down the road.

It's now six minutes before nine, and Mindy knows she's in trouble. Double trouble—from her dad and her mom. And I don't want to miss my match, but it might be too late.

"How did that man get that box up the bluff so quickly?" Mindy asks me.

"Like I said, a tunnel."

6

LATE AGAIN

PABLO

HIDING BEHIND PETER'S GRAY AND WHITE INFLATABLE BOAT, Mindy and I quickly decide on plan B. Plan A—to find my knife—was a total bust.

"It's better if you knock. Otherwise, it'll be weird, me asking," Mindy says.

I nod. Makes sense. However, I'm just about to knock when I hear Peter's voice.

"Hello . . . I'm over here," he calls out.

I run to the garage and find him grappling with a piece of equipment about his height with arms and legs and a helmet thing with pipes coming out of it.

"Glad you stopped by. Here. Help me with this JIM suit."

I grab the feet with lead weighs for soles. "What is it?" I ask.

"Keep going to the truck," he says out of breath, pointing with his chin.

We shuffle down the drive toward Mindy, who's standing in front of his boat so she can't be seen from the road.

"You're here too?" Peter asks.

She grabs the other foot. "Where's this going?" she asks.

"Here," he huffs. "One, two, three." We swing the thing over the side of the truck and it lands on the bed with a thud. "It's going to the lighthouse museum. During the Cold War, when we were listening for Russian subs in the Arctic, we used JIM suits like this to walk on the bottom to find mines."

"Couldn't the sub go to the bottom?" Mindy asks.

"Well, if the mine exploded, we'd loose the sub and everyone in it. So, the Navy would rather send down a diver as a sacrificial lamb. Anyway, everything's got to go—in the house, here, in the barn. I'm shipping out. It's all too much for me now."

Peter looks at our flushed faces. "What happened?" he asks. "You okay?"

We wipe the sweat from our foreheads, hesitating, not knowing what we should tell him.

I wave him off. "Oh, we're fine. Just running, you know. Training—"

"For soccer," Mindy fibs from those weeds again. "But now, Pablo's going to be late for his game, and I need to be at the hospital."

"The hospital? Are you okay?" Peter asks.

"Yes," she blurts. "My mom's at the Op Shop."

Peter rubs the gray stubble on his chin. I guess when you're his age you don't have to shave. He seems to have been wallowing in his thoughts, in the empty hours, listlessly counting down to that time when all his stuff is dealt with and he must leave his house and all its memories.

"Well, jump in, guys. Let's get you there ASAP."

Mindy and I exchange looks, hesitating. "It's okay," Mindy says. "My Mom's bought sunflowers from his farm stand."

We clamber into the cab of the truck, me next to Peter and

Mindy at the passenger window. "You've had your shots, right?" Peter asks.

We nod.

He puts on his mask—I guess just in case, and rolls down the windows. He skillfully reverses down the driveway with his boat on its trailer. As we come up to speed on the main road Peter steals a look at me. "And you, young man? Where do you need to be?"

"The park, next to the school, please," I say. Peter has seen the red scratches on my legs.

Next to me, Mindy is being quiet.

"So, did you have fun up there?"

We frown. Mindy adjusts her seatbelt.

"Well? You want to tell me about it?"

"The sound was great," Mindy says. "I thought I saw a zephyr but Pablo saw birds diving."

"I see." Peter says. He's been glancing at Mindy as she uses her spit to rub out a bramble scratch on her forearm. "So, FYI, I know how you got those bramble scratches," he says. "That property is covered in them. And I don't know why you need to go up there, but I suspect it has something to do with the tunnel. Am I right?"

We nod.

He nods thoughtfully. "That's what I thought. Well, you should know, my brother died there."

"How?" Mindy asks.

"Tainted bootleg liquor from Prohibition days. It's a long story, but stay away from that place."

I don't want to tell him we were trimming trees for the owner.

"The owner," he continues, "is someone you want to avoid. Take my word for it. Anyway . . . " He shoots Mindy a look. "Your dad? Does he also work in the emergency ward?"

She scowls at him. "What?"

27

"Oh, okay. So, what does he do?"

"He a doctor," she says, but then mumbles something under her breath.

"What's that?" Peter asks.

"He should go there," she says with a shaky voice.

"The ER? Why?"

"He's sick."

"Well, he's a doctor, right? So, he'll know when to go to the ER."

I can see Peter has not convinced Mindy. She squirms in her seat and now also glances at the inflatable boat on its trailer behind us.

"And you, young man, what's your name?" Peter asks.

"Pablo. Pablo Cruz."

"Like Pablo Picasso! You know who that is?"

"No." Once, Mom explained that I do actually have some similarities with the artist, but I don't want to discuss that with the old man—he'll make too much of it. And I wasn't named after the famous artist. I was named after a soccer player—and I'm not up for discussing that with him either. Mom said I'm short, speak Spanish, and am a foreigner like Picasso was when he studied in Italy. Even in France, when he was famous, he didn't act like he was French. But the main thing, Mom explained to me, is that I draw well. She found the characters I made up and asked me if I'd like to create a video game based on them. So, we started designing a game together.

I turn to Mindy to save me from having to explain all that.

"Mindy, please tell him your name," I whisper.

She scowls at me, then notices Peter's listening. "My name is Melinda," she says.

"So, let me guess, Melinda," Peter says. "Your mom works the ICU shift that ends at nine a.m. And right now, you're late. Call her. Tell her I'm dropping you off." He nods at her phone. "In fact, let me talk to her."

Peter thinks he's so smart guessing what Mrs. MacKay does, but he's wrong.

Mindy fidgets with the phone, then holds it to her ear. "Mom," she mutters, "I'll be there soon. A man is dropping me off. Yes, I know . . . I know! Here, he wants to talk to you." She stretches across me and offers her phone to Peter.

But Peter is driving and he shakes his head. "No, sorry, I can't take it. Pablo, hold the phone for me. I don't want that thing anywhere near my mouth. Put it on speaker."

Mindy activates the speaker and says to me, "Hold the phone for him."

"Who are you?" Mindy's mom squawks from the phone.

"Ma'am, this is Peter King," he says, projecting his voice. "I'm dropping off your daughter and her friend. I should be at the hospital in fifteen minutes."

"What's wrong with her? My daughter is in your car?"

"Ah, it's not a car. It's actually a red truck—an old Ford. She's fine. I'm towing my boat, so it's easy to spot when we pull into the parking lot."

"Mom, I'm fine—" Mindy chirps.

"Did you pick them up?" she asks Peter.

"They came to my house—"

"Your house!" she repeats. Mrs. McKay's voice has reached a gnarly high treble. Maybe it's the phone.

I glance at Mindy; she's rolling her eyes.

"To ask for a ride," he says.

I feel bad for Peter—this sounds nasty in so many ways. Mindy's mom is going ape, but that's what moms do to protect us. Or if we go missing.

"Mr. King, how long were they there?" she asks.

"Let me see...I heard the boy, Pablo—your daughter's friend—Pablo, say hello to the lady."

"Hello," I say, terrified I'll be blamed for Mindy's tardiness.

Peter smiles at me and continues. "He knocked on my front door, but I was in the garage at the time—"

"With my daughter?"

"No, Mom!" Mindy shouts, exasperated.

"Ma'am, if you let me finish . . . I'll remind you I'm talking to you on her phone—she called you. So, there's no need to be concerned. I'm driving now, and Mindy will be with you soon." He looks at us. "You guys were in a hurry to leave, right?"

"Yes," we both blurt.

But Mrs. MacKay is not done. "You're coming here now, right?"

"Just dropping Pablo at the soccer field. Then Mindy."

"No," she snaps back. "You drop Mindy first then him, okay?"

"It makes no difference to me," I say, though my match has started and Dad will be there looking for me.

Peter nods to thank me. "Okay," he says. "We'll be there soon."

"Thank you, Mr. King. I'll be waiting—"

"Yup," Peter interrupts. "Mindy, take me off the speaker."

Mindy brings her phone to her ear. She nods and sighs. "It's just . . . he has a soccer match." She listens with a slight nod or head shake, trying to respond to her mother's barrage of questions. "No, Mom! . . . Nothing! I know that . . . I have been with Pablo . . . I'll be there soon . . . Bye."

She looks up at Peter, then turns to me. "You should tell your coach you're late because you had a job."

∼

AFTER A WHILE OF LISTENING TO THE RATTLING GLOVE BOX DOOR in Peter's truck, he eventually puts on his indicator to turn left onto the hospital road. Mindy says. "Go straight."

Peter jerks his head back. "I thought you said she was at the hospital."

"No, I didn't. I said she's at the Op Shop—the hospital shop. Here," she says pointing.

He drives through the lot of parked cars to a cottage badly in need of a coat of paint. The sign painted on the window reads, *The Opportunity Shop*.

Peter's (and my) confusion is over—it seems Mindy's mother works at the thrift store.

We watch her short-cropped blond head storming toward us. Being at least six feet tall and fit means, she doesn't take long to get to the truck. She glares at Peter, who's turns to Mindy.

"Take care, Mindy," he says.

"Thank you," Mindy climbs out and slams the door behind her.

Her mother takes her hand without glancing at Peter and strides back to the Op Shop. "You're welcome," Peter mutters after them.

"She can't hear you," I say.

"Watch." Peter points at Mindy's mother. "Can't you hear what she's saying to her daughter? How disobedient she's been, and why hadn't she called, and how she needs to wise up before it's too late?"

I lean forward with my forehead on the window and watch

Mindy get smaller. But then she sneaks a glance back, and gives a wave with a quick shake of her other hand.

"You see? She did hear me," Peter says.

As Peter drives away I press an open hand on the window pane, but no one responds from inside the Op Shop.

THE OP SHOP

MINDY

AS PETER'S RED TRUCK AND BOAT SKULK OUT OF PARKING LOT like they've been punished, I realize what a decent man Peter was not to have argued with Mom; that's hard. Since meeting him early this morning Pablo and I have asked a lot of him, and he's been kind enough to help us with the ride. But now, I have to face three hours of watching Mom organizing everyone into a state of panic.

And of course, I'll be shown off to Mom's friends. Their sympathetic smiles reveal everything they think of her.

"Let go, Mom!" I say and pull my hand out of her grasp.

She steps in front of me. "I just wanted to get you away from that man and his truck." She smooths my hair and straightens my collar, treating me like a little girl. "I'm sorry, Mindy, but you should know better. Come. I've got a job for you."

I follow her to a rear area blocked off by a counter. A kindly, round-faced store volunteer takes a large black plastic bag from a woman who seems to have bagged her sorrows in it.

"We'll take it from here, ma'am. Thanks for donating to The Op Shop," the volunteer says.

The woman with mascara-streaked cheeks backs away and turns to leave.

The volunteer pulls clothing out of the bag. From what I can see they are men's clothes. She shakes her head and says, "Poor thing" as she inspects the jackets, shirts, and pants. Her white-gloved hands dart through the garments, examining a seam, frowning at a scuffed collar, or opening a shirt at arm's length.

Mom approaches, ushering me in front of her. "Sharon, I want you to meet Mindy," Mom says.

"Oh, Mindy, we've heard so much about you," Sharon says.

I can only imagine. "Nice to meet you, Sharon," I say.

"Darling," Mom says, "Call her Miss—" Mom clicks her fingers. "What *is* your last name Sharon?"

"Goodwin. Missus," she adds. "But you can call me Sharon, honey."

"So, I thought Mindy could help you stock shelves? I'll be finishing up in furniture if you need me. Mindy, stay here with Mrs. Goodwin."

If I wasn't observant, I wouldn't have noticed Sharon's eye roll, but considering I've just been delegated to her, she's being totally nice.

"How're you doin', hon?"

"Fine. What's that pile for?" I ask.

She shoots a quick glance at the pile on the floor. "Those are too icky to sell. The garments with frayed cuffs, stains and tears are thrown out. But they get recycled."

"Like compost?"

"No. They shred them for paper, I think. Better than the dump, right?"

"Definitely."

"So, Mindy, you see that pile of books over there?" She points to a linoleum countertop. "I want you to put them into the bookshelf down toward the front on the right. If there's a duplicate throw the worst one out. Okay?"

I nod. "Is there a sort order?"

Sharon shoots me a quizzical look. "Um…okay, let's say, alphabetical by last name of the author?" She's making it up.

I take a stack of books and stroll past the shelves of glasses, vases and bowls. These are what held the well-wishing flowers for the dead who never checked out of the hospital. In the center of the store, wide tables are piled with household items people no longer need. But someone does, because people are lining up at the cash register; there'll always be someone who wants a better home. A better life.

Sitting cross-legged in front of the bookcase I get depressed. It's a mess; bookshelves have to be logical. Now I understand Sharon's vague response about my sort-order question. Nevertheless, I decide to see how it works: Do I pick my top book and slot it into the alphabetically correct place, assuming there is one? Or do I sort the entire bookcase first? It doesn't matter, but I think they should be sorted by type. And so, I begin by placing my stack in the shelf, each book going next to one with a similar subject. It's suboptimal as Dad says, and doing this my way, I'm finding a lot of books on health—workout books, dieting, that sort of thing.

I'm guessing there's a reason I've noticed three books on yoga so far. I'm not surprised—these books seem to be for old people who throw them out because they lose interest. Or they die. Or they prefer the app. Yup, that's what I find when I google it. The covers have people in odd-looking positions with twisted necks, Indian people with perfect skin next to strange words like sutra, and drawings of the tree of life. I'm about to put a duplicate aside when I flip it open to a page with a phrase that hooks me in: *pain relief*. I read a little before and after the phrase and now realize this might be the answer to Dad's problem.

"How's it going?" It's Mom. She's wielding a wok like the shield of a Nordic goddess.

"Okay, I guess. Putting books away."

"Find anything interesting?"

I hold up the book on yoga. "Do you think Dad would try yoga?"

She makes one of those short ear-numbing laughs. "Don't be silly, dear."

How can I tell her that yoga is used for pain relief when I don't know what I'm talking about? But I do know this: I'm only *silly* when I want to be. "Are you going to bonk someone upside the head with that wok?" I ask.

She gives me a slight smile as she wags her finger at me and goes off to organize kitchen things. This place is perfect for her. She means well—and she's a good mom, but does she have to be so annoying? Man!

I just want to help Dad past his pain—if he'd only try it. Try anything other than drugs.

Sharon appears when I'm finishing up the chapter. "Mindy? Done yet?"

Mom has sent her to check on me. It's obvious.

"Well, I've been sorting by type of book as I go. I've got love stories here, and here are stories like adventure, and down here are the books for making things. Tables. Fixing things…this one on how to fix leaking pipes, seems good."

"That's nice, Mindy. Now come and get some more. What's that one?" She points to the book I set aside.

"It's a duplicate."

"Give it to me. I'll toss it for you."

"Can I keep it?"

"Oh, sure. Yeah, yeah. But I need that pile gone. Okay?"

I shove the last three books into the bookcase and return to the counter where I wedge the yoga book into the bottom of the pile. Then I take the next stack to the bookcase and repeat my task.

Presently, Mom approaches wearing a flippant smile. "Hey. Sorry about that. Want to get a coffee?"

"No, but I really need breakfast," I gasp when I see it is only ten thirty on what promises to be the longest Saturday of my life.

I'm now seriously ravenous.

WE STRIDE DOWN TO THE BAKERY—NORMAL WALKING IS ALMOST impossible for her. But her pace works for me because I'm desperate for the soft buttery crunch of a chocolate croissant in my mouth.

Inside it smells of freshly baked bread. Mom peers through the display glass at the pastries, cakes, and croissants. She hands over her credit card and orders croissants—plain for her, chocolate for me. We find a little table by the window. Mom looks like she's about to play house with dolls.

"Didn't you have breakfast?" she asks.

I'm about to lie to her about the geography project, when the cashier says her cappuccino is ready.

"Ah. Coffee. Hold that thought. I ordered a smoothie for you."

She knows I like them because Dad makes them on Saturdays —at least he used to. Which reminds me. I run to the counter.

"Mom, I have to go back. I left my book there. I'll be right back. Someone will take it."

"Mindy, slow down. Get it on Kindle."

I'm half out the door when she calls after me. "Come back here."

"No. I'll be right back. Hold that thought." I have to be firm to get my way with Mom.

"Well . . . okay. Hurry," Mom says, like it's her idea.

As I run past the bake shop window I see her sitting at the little table. She's looking into her coffee as she stirs. My heart goes out to her, but I know that Dad will never open a Kindle book—especially not one on yoga, and especially not when he is desperate for a pain pill. However, if he keeps the book by his bedside table, he might, just might, open it to my sticky-noted chapter on pain management. The book will be a last reminder to him that I miss him—and so does Mom—before he blasts into black space and forgets there are people who love him.

I run faster. She's sitting there alone, wondering about me and about why we don't get along. With no one to boss around, she's withdrawn into herself. I could ask her why she bullies everyone, but I know why: she blames herself for Dad not getting better, for not getting closer to me. I can't blame her and I don't want to hurt her feelings or take out my revenge for her insensitive ways.

It's clear to me now that the job she had for me at the Op Shop was to make her feel like she had a daughter who loved her.

But she forgot to give me that job.

8

THE GIFT

PABLO

AT THE TOWN SPORTS FIELDS PETER PULLS UP TO THE CURB; THE parking spots are too small for his truck and trailer. From here we have a view of the soccer match—and, with possession of the ball, whoever that is playing my left wing position is pretty good. That should be me. Dad is on the field, refereeing the game.

"Well, this is you, my friend," Peter says. "I'm sorry you missed your game, Pablo. You want me to stick around while you check to see if you have a ride?"

"No thanks. That referee is my dad."

And yeah, this *is* me, sitting here on the sidelines, watching him.

Peter's raised bushy eyebrows show he expects me to jump out of the truck, like Mindy did. But there's so much more I want to know about him, and this might be the last time I see him. What will he do next? Go home to that house to pack boxes? Pack up his life? Getting ready to ship out, as he said. "Why can't you keep your boat?" I ask.

"I suppose I could berth it at a marina, but what's the point? I never take her out anymore. Why do you ask?"

39

Peter is not only losing his house; he's losing his boat. I twist around to look back at the inflatable. He'll never fish again. He'll miss breathing in the salt air, the sting of spray on his face, and his bones will forget the solid roll of the swell. And now he's giving this up. For what?

"Don't you have family to help you pack?" I ask.

"My son and daughter have moved away—my son to California, my daughter to the UK. She ran off with an Englishman. So, I split the difference and stay on here, on the East Coast. I do have some friends with the Audubon Society; I like birds. That's why I bought the inflatable boat. But everyone's too busy...or dying."

"There were fish in the sound," I say. "I saw the ruffle."

"Oh yeah?"

"Mindy thought it was a zephyr but the birds were diving for porgies—it's that time of year."

"What else is good to catch at this time of year?" he asks.

"Fluke, blues, maybe a striper."

"Yup. You're a fisherman."

"My dad is."

"And, does your mom go too?"

"Sometimes. But she studies a lot, and also has a job at Ke's Laundry, ironing shirts."

Peter's staring at the soccer field watching the game. It seems his thoughts are far away. My life seems so much better than his. How does a man become so sad? It's hard to say who is to blame. Maybe no one. It's just like that when you get old.

"Peter?"

The old man pulls his eyes off the match and comes back to the present. "Oh . . . yes, okay Pablo," he says, as if he's seeing me for the first time. "It was nice to meet you. Good luck."

"You should go out. One last time." I point my thumb over my shoulder at the boat.

"Why? Go. It's halftime. Your dad is looking for you."

I open the door and then face him. "Okay, but there's good fishing today."

"You want to go out, don't you?" he asks.

I want to answer, but it's obvious, so I slam the passenger door and trot over to Dad, who's waving at me.

"Pablo," I hear Peter calling. He comes around the front of his truck taking his time walk to walk toward me.

"Come out with me on the boat," he heaves. "I'd like to give something to your new American family, before I capitulate to the uncompromising hand of time. This might be your lucky day, but only if your dad agrees."

Yes! A final outing for Peter. "Wait. I'll ask Dad—*he* must also capitulate to the uncompromising hand of time, whatever that means."

"It means, never say never. So, go. I'm going to drive over to the lighthouse to drop off the Jim Suit. I'll swing by after the match."

DAD THROWS UP HIS HANDS AS I APPROACH. "WHAT HAPPENED TO you?"

It's time for me to tell the truth. "I went to look for the knife you gave me."

"I know you dropped it, but I thought you picked it up."

"No. I'm sorry, Dad. I couldn't find it."

"That's a pity, but the main thing is, you went back for it—I see the scratches from the brambles up there on the slope." He wipes the sweat off his face with a towel. "That shows me you saw it as more than just a gift. I should have said when I gave it to you that it was my way of saying you can face your own challenges. Like on the knife, some problems need to be cut; or screwed in or out; or have a hole punched through them; or hooked so you can get them back." He pats my shoulder.

He knows my school has information that threatens to uproot us once again: He could be called on to explain my poor grades, the one or two friends I have—not counting Mindy, which they don't, and my truancy, which could lead to questions about my Dreamer status and could spilt our family apart. That was a constant fear in California.

He wipes the back of his neck and looks up. "You know, Pablo, it was wrong of me to keep you out of school yesterday. We can have a good life here."

"But what about the winter, when you can't work?"

"Sure, there are days in winter when the trees ice over. But those days are kinder than those Fresno winds that blew off the Sierra Nevadas."

I remember. He would come home covered in dust from picking broccoli with his sweat frozen on his hands. His forgiveness means a lot to me. "I will find it," I say.

"Well," he continues, "whatever problem you have, you can solve it when you have the right tools—not only on the knife; those tools work best when they're in your head. I know you know that."

I nod, but I have not told the full truth because I don't know what that nasty guy with pointy boots was up to. I'll have to explain it to Dad sooner or later.

"Or, maybe you won't find it," Dad continues. "Hey, we all make mistakes. But sometimes mistakes can't be fixed, so it's best not to make them. Now, who's the old goat with the boat?"

"Peter—the sunflower farmer next to that property. He gave us a ride."

"Us?" Dad blinks.

"Mindy and me. Anyway, he wants to go fishing one last time before he sells his boat and asked if we could go with him, 'cause . . . as you can see, he's old."

Dad checks his watch. "Halftime's over. But yes, tell him we'll go after the match."

9

THE DROP DOOR

PABLO

IT'S A BUMPY RIDE THROUGH THE CHOPPY WATERS OF THE SOUND IN Peter's twelve-foot rigid inflatable boat, which he shortens to RIB. Dad looks back at the shore kind of nervous. He prefers fishing off the rocks or the beach.

Peter follows Dad's glances back at the shore. "Fred, it's impossible to make out the navigational markers along these jagged coastal bluffs. Regulars look for a tall copse of northern red oaks. One tree is much taller . . . " He squints his eyes at the bluffs. "That's funny, I don't see it now. It's a landmark on the skyline for boaters who want to take the inlet that comes out into the marina."

Dad doesn't think it's funny. He knows we were trimming trees exactly where Peter is looking up at the bluff. He knows I cut the top off that tall tree, and now we know there was a reason—we just don't know why. We lean forward to keep the bow down. He pokes a finger into the side of the boat and shakes his head.

"It's Hypalon. Don't worry about it—you're safe," Peter shouts.

We've caught some porgies and Peter is headed for the inlet. When he eases the throttle to five miles an hour, he beckons Dad over. "Check this out—just to show you how safe this boat is." Peter idles the motor. He unscrews the cover to one of the valves to show how it's pumped. He presses the valve in, releasing a blast of air that stops when he lets go.

I feel the boat keen to one side, but Peter calmly inflates the section with a foot pump. As he returns the pump to the hatch, I see a phone in a labeled Ziploc bag. "That's the password for your phone?" I ask, pointing at the bag.

"Yes, I always store my phone like this—powered down for emergencies and the password on the bag for someone to call if I can't call."

Dad nods approvingly.

"You can use the boat whenever you like," Peter says. "In fact, keep it. They'll just rack it at the marine sales place, you know? I won't get much after their take, and I hate to think someone will use my RIB to get to their yacht and back. So…it's yours."

"Too expensive," Dad says, shaking his head.

"No. Gratis."

"Yeah!" I say and throw my hands in the air. My mind is racing. We'll have free fish and Mom can make that red snapper dish with parsley cream, garlic, and lime juice.

Dad smiles at me and faces Peter.

"*Muchas gracias*," he says.

"*De nada*, Fred, " Peter says. "Sorry, I never learned Spanish. Say, you want to get lunch?"

Dad beams and gives a thumbs-up.

"I always have an appetite for high-carb diner food after fishing—and I know exactly where to get it. If this is to be my last run, then let's finish it with a slobber-fest," Peter says. "You can have a cowboy with spurs, blowout patches, and an eve with a lid."

Dad and I look at him. He's talking another language—and it's not English.

Peter smiles. "That, my friends, is diner speak for a western omelet with fries, pancakes and a slice of apple pie. What do you say, Pablo?"

It's not just English I have to learn, now it's diner speak as well.

"I say, I'm hungry," I reply.

"Well, let's go." He navigates up the inlet past the tour operators and boat dealerships that line the bank. "I've plied these waters for so many years—never changes." He slows as we approach the old mill Mindy and I saw from the top of the ridge. Peter glides to the rotted deck of the mill and begins to tether the boat.

Suddenly my heart is pumping blood so hard I feel like I'll burst. I want to tell him that the truck that chased us down to his house was carrying a red box from a fishing boat that tied up to the mill. I reject the idea that Peter could be involved as soon as I get it. Those were bad guys we saw, but I can't tell Peter or Dad now because they'll never believe me. Dad will think I'm confusing boats that were getting gas next to the mill—because it was supposed to look that way. And Peter will just know it didn't happen because he's been around the deserted mill for so long. There was no crime. If I had hard evidence, I would have told them sooner.

Out of the boat, Dad and I watch Peter thoughtfully running his eyes over the mill. He strolls over the stark, buckled deck. A moldy concrete umbrella stand is all that remains. The salt winds coming off the sound have etched the windowpanes with grime. The upper-level windows have been boarded up more recently so someone

46

must care enough to stop the winter storms from ripping through the upper windows, gutting the roof, and turning the mill into a pile of lumber.

I chicken out and ask, "Are we going to eat?"

"Sure. But let me tell you something about this place," Peter says. "In 1969, thirty-six years after Prohibition ended in New York State, my brother died here, of alcoholic poisoning."

"I'm sorry," Dad says.

Peter nods and continues. "It was a time of free love and free drugs, but we were in the Navy and too busy getting drunk to find time for drugs—but we were committed drinkers. Herman and I came here because our dad used to get his supplies for his speakeasy from the mill. The checkpoints along the Long Island highway never apprehended the bootleggers because the mill was a major supplier to local joints and up-island to Manhattan.

"While we were on crew shore leave off the submarine, we found a case of hidden 'hooch' in the tunnel under the mill—hidden for good reason, we found out. Herman took just one sip—for the hell of it. Killed him."

So, he knows about the tunnel. I need to warn him. "We need to leave, Peter. It's dangerous here—"

"Nah, that was a long time ago." He looks up at the old mill. "I must never forget this. Its tragedy is bored into its clapboard past; it's weathered, but it's not forgotten. And thank you guys for coming out with me because I can now see it one last time. We can go inside here. The street side is boarded up. You coming?"

Around the back, along a thin walkway ledge facing the water, Peter sees a door. There are foot tracks coming and going. The mill is not deserted. A cleverly hidden power cable has been extended from a warehouse in the boatyard next door.

"They must be working inside," Dad says.

"I don't see construction workers," I say.

Peter holds his finger up to his lips and whispers, "Stop. Observe. Listen. It's a habit I learned on the submarine. This spot would have been where they took deliveries of fish and produce from boats, perhaps in exchange for milled wheat to be ground by the mill."

He beckons us to follow him in, though he's cautious.

Peter points at the gutted interior. In a low voice he says, "They converted it into a restaurant after the mill closed."

As we step into the service kitchen area, we hear voices coming from the floor above. Now I see the power cable running up the staircase. I smell something acrid in the air. We skulk into a storage room that must have once served as a larder, its shelves long since emptied. Peter eases the door closed on rusted hinges, leaving it cracked. I peer through, hearing the voices better.

Peter whispers close to my ear as we both spy through the crack in the door. "What are they saying?"

"Someone stole . . . something," I say softly.

One of the voices rises in protest and screams, "No!" We hear a thump. Someone heaving. A chair scrapes, falls. Heavy footfalls pound the floorboards above us. A desperate bellow is followed by what sounds like a body tumbling down the staircase. We hear two maybe three men coming down the stairs.

The last is obviously the boss—a tall sunburned dude with long, greasy black hair over the collar of his mottled military camo jacket. But what scares me most is the scar running across his forehead, ending in his right eye socket—a black hole. He is uglier than a sockeye salmon.

Before Dad can pull me away from the crack in the door, I see a man's body being dragged, its boots scraping along the floorboards leading into the kitchen area—toward us. The two men dragging the body stop in front of the larder.

We freeze. My breathing sounds like a hurricane to me. All I see are his pants and shoes. But then the body is dragged away and I see a face—a bald white man, older than Dad, barely alive.

10

ESCAPE

PABLO

I HAVE SEEN ENOUGH TO KNOW THAT NOW IS THE TIME TO USE THE tools in my head.

Peter has put us in danger. He is too curious for his own good, and he has made a mistake. Dad was right—some mistakes can't be fixed. Like this one.

The larder we're hiding in has a small high sash window to let in the light, and I'm guessing for ventilation. I tap Dad's shoulder and mime the leg up he needs to give me so I can crawl through. Dad scowls at me, wagging is finger.

"I can get help," I whisper back fiercely. "It's wrong to be here knowing someone is getting murdered."

Dad and Peter exchange looks. They know if we leave the larder and get caught, it will not go well for us. They lift me up to the narrow window. On the other side, I see a drop of about eight feet. I shake my head and they bring me down.

Peter peers back through the crack in the door and returns, more worried than before. "He might have seen me." Peter says. With quick and quiet instructions, Peter urges Dad to get me onto his shoulders. Tentatively, Dad places his foot into Peter's cradled hands and hoists me over the mantle of the window. Once through, he lowers me, then lets go. I land softly, just like I do in soccer.

I crouch against the clapboard outside wall of the mill on the narrow walkway. Below me the fast-moving outgoing tide slides under the mill. I hear someone moaning. Choking. Something grinds on old hinges. There's a splash. A shout from under the mill.

I lie on my stomach with my head inches above the rushing water so I can see underneath. A maze of pilings supports the building, and about twelve feet from where I am, I see a door gaping open to the water. Peter said they took deliveries in exchange for milled wheat—it's a drop door, maybe to get rid of the chaff. There's a rope coming out of it. On the other end, something large is moving. It's the bald man with the other end of the rope tied around his neck. He is swiveling and treading water without using his hands, which are tied behind his back. He's gasping for air as the water flows over his face and up his nose. He pleads for his life, and it's Sockeye, I'm sure, who's taunting him.

"Now you can think about what happens when you steal from us…maybe I leave you down there. Or maybe we force you to work on the factory ship…for the rest of your life. We know where your family is, Doctor, but they'll never know where you are. I should put a bullet through that shiny thick head of yours."

I need to run away as fast as I can. But Sockeye bursts through the outside kitchen door—the same door we came through earlier. I have no way to escape, except down into the water. I slide quietly over the edge of the walkway and drop into the cool, strong current.

I hang onto a piling and listen for Sockeye to pass overhead. Nothing happens. Instead, I hear the grumbling motors of a launch start up. Sockeye is leaving. He'll see Peter's boat tied to the deck and want to know why it's there. Peter's boat needs to disappear—fast—before Sockeye takes off.

I let the current carry me one piling at a time toward the RIB. But I have a problem. Do I help this man tied to the pier? He's going to drown. I thought I heard Sockeye say he's a doctor. Or do I hide the boat so Dad and Peter are not caught in the larder?

It's an easy choice; family comes first.

I let the current float me to the next piling. Doctor Bald is still treading water, spluttering with that rope around his neck.

I can't do it—I can't pass by him.

I pull the man toward me using the rope, which chokes him even worse. The knot in the rope around his neck is too tight to untie. If I had my pocketknife with me, I'd easily cut the rope and free him—if he was still alive.

"Wrap your legs around this piling," I say. "Put your back to the current so you can keep you head up." It's not up to me to decide if he's guilty of stealing or not. And if he *is* stealing, is he one of the good guys stealing from bad guys? And what kind of doctor is he?

"Thank you," he pants, "but I don't know long my legs will hold on before I let go."

"Nor do I. I'm going to get help," I lie. It's urgent I move Peter's boat first.

I let the current take me past the pilings and maneuver to collide with Peter's boat. Due to the loose knot, I easily untether the boat and float it under the deck toward the bank, but it catches on the beams.

Peter deflated the boat earlier. I do the same with all three air valves until it is barely keeping the outboard motor above water. Then I float it to the bank and jam it between the bank and the decking. This way, we'll be able to retrieve it when Dad and Peter have escaped the mill.

Sockeye roars away in the fishing boat I saw earlier. I know he hasn't seen me under the deck because of his unseeing black eye socket is facing me. With that face it's not hard to imagine that eye getting gouged out in a knife fight. If I worked for him, I'd be terrified, which is probably why I have not heard from the other two men who were with him. Maybe he told them to stay upstairs and continue their work. Doing what, I don't know, but it means Dad and Peter cannot leave. There's no way I can go back inside the mill, so I must get help from the outside.

I feel my phone in my pocket. Wouldn't that be nice? It's supposed to be submersible down to nineteen feet, so I try it. It lights up. I open the phone app. Who do I call? I can't call Dad because I'll blow his cover. Mom's training for the marathon with her running club, but I call anyway. No answer. I don't leave a message, but I text, *Gone fishing with Dad.* I do not want to alarm her.

Mindy can't really help me. I know her: she'll advise, recommend, and reassure me, and that's great normally, but I need to get Dad and Peter out of that mill—now.

I'm out of options and time. I need to act. I call.

"Mindy?" I say softly.

"It's a bad connection, Pablo," she says. "Text me."

I text, *@mill. We can't leave*

She texts back, *You ok? We?*

Dad and Peter. Please help. But don't call the cops!

I wait for a reply, realizing what I am asking her to do—get help, but not official help, because Dad doesn't have permanent legal status in the US. In the meantime, my legs are turning into ice from the cool current. I have to move. I know the tunnel under the mill doesn't start under the deck. I need to know where it starts. I know where it ends, though—at the top of the bluff, where my pocketknife lies.

I swim under water until I have cleared the deck overhead and then haul myself up onto the bulkhead at the side of the service road. I dart across to the tower structure, hoping no one sees me.

The door is open. It seems to have been used at some point as a marine workshop that repaired boating and fishing gear. Above me is a corrugated steel tank with a broken pipe coming out of the bottom. Of course—it's an old rusted-through tank that once supplied water to the mill across the road.

To get a better view of how the water came into the tank I squeeze past an old outboard motor with its cover off. The pipe that fed the water to the tank comes out of a wide hole in the roof on the side that abuts the bluff. The shaft is wide enough for people to climb up.

I've found the tunnel—an escape from the mill, and in the past, a way to smuggle bootleg liquor out.

As my eyes adjust, I notice a shiny steel cable also coming out of the tunnel. It's attached to a fishing net hidden by the bric-a-brac of the workshop. In it is a red fishing tackle box, just like the one the man in the truck fetched from the hole in the top of the bluff, just like the one we saw Sockeye bring into the mill.

I open the box and see a tray of jig head hooks, fishing lures, and assorted sinkers, weights, and floats. Really? A fishing box? I lift out the tray and find the answer to all the questions pounding in my head.

Pills.

They are not the round ones, but tube-like capsules—one half, light-brown, one half, green. In Ziploc bags.

I snap the tray back in place and shut the lid. I've watched CSI on TV and know there'll be fingerprints on those bags. I've also watched TV shows with Dad about the drug gangs. Nothing like what he and Mom ran from—the cartels were far worse; they killed many of Mom's relatives. So Dad brought his family with him to the US. "We all go," he had said. And now here I am, mixed up with the same evil.

I lean in and look up the shaft that goes through the bluff. To the side of it I see footholds made from rebar in the form of giant staples driven into the side of the bluff.

This is no time to overthink. I can't wait to see if Mindy does anything about my texts. I must get help without calling and the best way to leave is through the tunnel.

As I climb up the tunnel I am driven by the thought of Dad with the barrel of a gun in his face, and Peter with a blade at his throat, and the bald man drowning in the current. Another nasty thought comes to me: my fingerprints, and maybe Dad's, will be on the pocketknife. If they find it and dust for prints they'll suspect we're working with the doctor.

When I get to the top, all I have to do is nudge the thing they use to cover the hole.

It doesn't move. It's heavy and metal and doesn't even budge a little. I didn't see it last night, but I do remember the truck dude using a winch—and it wasn't to haul up a fishing box that weighs less than a pound. I try again, but it won't move.

Dad is relying on me. Yet, here I am, stuck in the smuggling tunnel.

I hear voices approaching below. Spanish words. I smell cigarette smoke. The door opens to the light of day, throwing shadows across the lighted side of the tunnel, cast from the men entering. I can barely make out the low murmuring, except possibly about fetching something. These gang guys get away with this by posing as fishermen. It's all connected and out of sight—no vehicles, no people, no coming and going. To the casual onlooker the mill is forgotten.

It's anything but.

It seems everyone is waiting for me to do something. The weight of my body rests on the thin rebar. I feel my feet going numb.

SOMETHING FUNNY ABOUT THE MIIL

MINDY

MOM, HAVING FINISHED HER (AND THEREFORE ALSO MY) SIX-HOUR shift at the Op Shop, has stopped to get gas—full service. She's applying lipgloss and says, "Thing is, I could get a grant for the Op Shop—spruce it up a bit, but as long as it looks like it's amateur night—"

The ring of my phone cuts her short. She stares at me.

"Excuse me, Mom. Sorry. It's Pablo," I say.

"I know. Put it away, Mindy."

"Let me take a quick look. Please?"

She glares at me with narrowed eyes. "Go ahead."

When Pablo whispers my name like a question, I know right away something's wrong. I tell him to text and hang up.

My phone vibrates.

His text reads, @*mill. We can't leave*

This makes no sense. How many goals did he score at his match and what is he doing at the mill? And the real question is, who is *we*?

But mom is eyeballing me. I text, *You ok? We?*

The text shoots back. *Dad and Peter. Please help. But don't call the cops!*

Of course, I won't. I know his dad is living in the US illegally.

Mom grabs the phone right out of my hand and reads. She places it facedown in her lap. "Mindy, what's going on here? What has your little Dreamer friend gotten himself into—hiding things from the cops?"

"I don't know!" I say. "And he's not my little friend, he's my friend—you're so—"

"So what, Mindy? Protective? Caring? Concerned for your safety?" She shakes her head as she hands her credit card to the attendant. "I don't want you to end up like Troy—what was his last name?"

"Gillis. I knew him...an all-state pick as a sophomore in 2020, second in the state with 127 tackles that led our school district to a division one state runner-up finish. That's not me. The point is, you judge Pablo."

"I do, I know. Sorry, I shouldn't have said that. Now tell me, who's Peter?"

"You met him. The old man who gave us a ride."

"Him? What would that old man want with that boy? Did you ask yourself that?"

"He's not a perv, Mom! You really should meet with him. You'd see that he's kind and really is not trying to make trouble."

"Yeah, I'm not meeting with him. In fact, I'm calling 911," she says under her breath.

She fishes into her bag and pulls out her phone.

"Mom, don't!" This is what troubles me: she doesn't trust me; she's not a trusting person. She keeps everyone away from me.

"Something's going on, Mindy. Your friend is in trouble and that mill is a nasty place . . . Yes, hello, operator? Yes, I'm reporting a child in trouble . . . I don't know the situation. We—my daughter actually, got a text from him saying they can't leave. Pablo . . . twelve years old."

"Cruz," I butt in, then immediately regret it. Have I just betrayed him?

She rolls her eyes. "Pablo Cruz. He's with an old man...I don't know him...they're at the mill down at the inlet. Okay. Thank you."

Unfreaking believable. Some friend I am.

"Why did you do that? Pablo'll never trust me again."

"Yes, he will."

I sigh. "You know, Mom, being tall and pushy doesn't make you right all the time. I watched you today, running around, organizing the volunteers like you're in charge, but you're a volunteer just like them. So, who gave you that job?"

"Are you finished?"

"Yes."

As she pulls out of the gas station she says, "Tall, pushy, and don't forget about smart. You should try it; think of it as empowerment. And now, let's go watch the fun at the mill."

Oh joy—irony. She's so happy, she's irresponsible. She'll probably boss around the rescue party and EMTs.

When she pulls into the traffic, I text Pablo again: *Mom's called the cops. Run*

1 2

MISSING

PABLO

THERE'S NOWHERE TO GO BUT DOWN. MY USUAL SPEED AND agility are as useless as are the tools inside my head.

I climb down the tunnel, rung by careful rung and get a clearer view of the shadowy figures whose whispered fragments of words sound more urgent.

At the top of the water tank, I peer through a rusted hole. The dry bottom has an opening that once connected the supply pipe to the mill across the street.

Far-off sirens wail in the distance. Did Mindy misread my text?

I spot daylight streaming through a missing roof tile and remember now that the tower is built right next to the bluff. I can smell grass and leaves. I hear a rustling. I move closer to the hole. For a moment I don't know what I'm looking at.

It's the barrel of sniper's rifle.

I shift. The scope is aimed at the upper-floor window of the mill by an officer in a uniform I don't recognize.

"Señor," I whisper through the hole in the roof.

The barrel whips around and points between my eyes.

"Help me."

The barrel lowers. The sniper radios. "This is Three. Boy located, stand by."

Inside, there's a movement below the tank. An interchange of light reveals a red box being pushed through the hole and moved out of sight. Men are still down there, hiding from Sockeye, which is a really bad idea.

"Sir, there are men down here."

"Stay where you are, son." The sniper radios in, giving the go command.

On the street below, police cruisers and armored trucks have surrounded the mill. I doubt the people below hear the report of the sniper's rifle, but it seems to have set off series of explosions on the upper floor of the mill. Or could the fire have been started by the men who come out with their hands over their heads, to destroy the evidence?

The bullhorn is blaring commands as thick white smoke billows through the upper-floor window and blows in my direction. Flames lick the clapboard. It smells of chemicals. My throat constricts and my heart pounds. I should not be breathing it in.

I'm uncertain if Dad and Peter are in there. Were they found by the men upstairs? Did the doctor drown?

A police radio squawks again and I see Peter and then Dad emerge from the mill's entrance door with their hands raised. They are told to kneel with their hands behind their heads. Town cops handcuff them. As they are led away, a female plainclothes police officer intervenes to question Peter.

Dad is led toward a cruiser. His head is pushed down as he's forced into the back seat.

Peter points to where his boat was tied up, but of course it's not there. Which means the woman detective is probably asking what they were doing there and where the boy is. She uncuffs him and hands Peter her card. The cruiser with Dad in it drives off.

This does not look right, and I am to blame. I am directly responsible for Dad's arrest. I have broken my promise to him to get help. I will make it up to him.

In the tower below a SWAT team rushes in. There's a chaos of activity: police and radios blaring and harsh words at the men who've been stealing from Sockeye. I remain still as the arrests are made, and when they all finally leave, I give it a minute before I move.

The cable is sliding up the shaft again, hoisting the net with another tackle box in it. At the top I hear the plate scrape, and then the roar of the pickup as it pulls away from the pit. The shaft has been left open.

Now I have a chance to save Dad. As long as I am missing the police will not hand him over to Immigration. This time, I shimmy up the tunnel and out into the late afternoon light of the forest.

I'm missing—and that's the way it has to be. For now.

13

EMPOWERMENT

MINDY

W HEN M OM AND I ARRIVE AT THE MILL THE POLICE HAVE ALREADY cordoned off the area. She parks some distance away from the mill, in the parking lot for the tour boat people. The police cars are from our town, but others say *Sheriff*. Some are black, bigger, stronger-looking things. There's even an SUV-type van with grills over the windows. A very cross cop with a bullhorn is shouting at the mill —though I can't make out a word he's saying.

"Now what?" Mom asks, drumming her fingers on the steering wheel. "Where is he? Your little friend?"

I shake my head, but say nothing—she'll never understand him. I stare over the inlet and watch two police patrol vessels directing boat traffic around the mill. Pablo knows the one place they might not know about—the tunnel to the hole at the top of the buff. So why did he say, *We can't leave*?

"There," I point through random law enforcement vehicles. Peter is pointing to the deck of the mill, to a woman—a detective, maybe—who's listening and making notes. She hands him her card.

I open the car door.

"No, Min." Mom shakes her head and her finger like they're connected. "Let them do their job."

"That's Peter," I point. "The man who gave us the ride. And, by the way, you do know him; you bought sunflowers at his farm stand."

She nods. "That's the man? I knew he was no good."

She drums her fingers on the steering wheel. For her, the world does not spin fast enough, and Peter, who grinds slow and steady, is a stone in her shoe.

Thing is, I know Pablo's around here. His text said he was with his father and Peter, but why? And if they're questioning Peter, why aren't they questioning Pablo's dad?

I get back in the car, but I feel Pablo's presence. Like he's looking at me.

Smoke is coming out of the top window of the mill, wafting up the bluff, which is where Pablo might be hiding. Officers are walking two handcuffed men to the police van. They're a rough-looking bunch and almost definitely Latino.

"Well, clearly there's a lot more going on here," Mom says, getting out. "Come. Stick with me. Let's find out from him." She points at a cop on duty by the van.

He watches us approach.

"Officer." She nods at him. "Who's in charge? My daughter reported the missing boy."

"What boy? Please step back, ma'am."

"You should call your superior. He'll know." Mom turns her back on the officer and faces me. "Have you been here before?

"No. But we saw it from the top of the ridge." A half-lie. "That's when we met Peter."

She's about to say something snide, but the officer is getting something on his shoulder radio. Then says to Mom, "They've found the boy." He tells her. "So's you know."

I grind my heel into the gravel. This is not what Pablo wanted. Now they can send his father back to Mexico—at least, I think that's what he was trying to avoid. Still, I'm glad he wasn't caught in the fire. He's like a cat at the circus darting between the legs of the elephants, tempting them to step on him. But he's wily—now you see him, now you don't.

The cop is frowning at me. "Are you family?"

"No," I say. "He's my friend. It's just that . . . well, you should know that he's protected by the DACA policy."

"What is *dacca*," he asks, leaning down to hear me better.

"The Development, Relief, and Education for Alien Minors Act, also known as the DREAM Act. He has the right to work."

"Is that what he was doing here? Working? Yes, he does have the right to work—provided it's legal."

Mom has been watching me. I have to believe she's actually impressed that I know this.

The officer pulls a notepad out and turns to Mom. "Name and phone please. In case we have questions."

"MacKay, Penelope. My daughter is Melinda." Mom watches him misspell our last name. "M-A-C-K-A-Y," she corrects, then says, "I go by Penny." Then gives him our address and phone number.

"Anything else you can tell us?" he asks.

"Like what? The boy is apparently found. His family will be relieved."

Returning to the car, Mom asks, "How come you know this immigration stuff? I thought you did well, defending your friend."

"He needed to know. So I spoke up. I think of it as empowerment—without being pushy."

Mom sneaks out a chuckle and smiles. "That's my girl. Let's pick up a pizza."

14

THE GLOVE OF LIGHT

PABLO

UNTIL I FIGURE OUT HOW TO DISAPPEAR, I DECIDE TO USE PETER'S garage. Getting in is a no-brainer because the side door is not locked. Besides, his truck isn't in the drive. But now I hear him pull in and open the back door. I knew he wouldn't put the truck in the garage because he can't—it's filled with half-filled boxes for his move.

I could go home. But that will force Mom to hide me from everyone—if she agrees that I should stay missing. But of course, she won't—she'll work something else out because she's a lot smarter and braver than me. I could support her in her crazed panic to find Dad somewhere in law enforcement land. The authorities will hold Dad, perhaps for gathering evidence, or at worst, suspecting he's part of the gang.

As I think through my options of how to get home, sitting here in the shorts and the tee-shirt I had on early this morning, rubbing my dirty, sore feet, I smell fried meat and onions that fire a hunger like I've never felt before. Whether it's the prospect of food or Peter's understanding, I decide to ask for his help.

I knock. Then a little harder.

"Just a minute," I hear from the kitchen.

He opens the door and takes a good look at me.

"Pablo. I knew you were a survivor. Come in. I was just eating. You hungry?"

"Yes, Mr. Peter."

"Just Peter, please. Drop the mister. Now come." He points down the passage. "There's the bathroom. Wash your hands. And your face. I'll have food ready for you."

He sits me at the kitchen table with a plate of sausages and leeks, then drops a piece of steamed broccoli on it. "Eat. I made enough for lunch tomorrow because I'll be packing, so dig in."

He watches me eat and then gets a paper towel. "Here," he says. "Wipe your mouth."

After a long drink of water, I say. "I can't go home."

Peter nods. "Eat, my friend. Don't try to talk. Then you can tell me everything."

When I've finally had enough, he says, "So what happened after your dad dropped you out of the window?"

"I had to do something. So, I helped the doctor stay afloat, then I moved the RIB, then I decided to escape through the tunnel. But I got stuck."

"Wow," he says. "That's quite a day. Do you see your power? It's like a hand inside a glove of light."

"What does that mean?" I ask.

Peter looks down and clenches his fist then flexes his fingers in front of my eyes. "Power is what drives our actions—it's like a hand that does things we don't notice. But our hands don't work well if we cannot see. In the dark hands can act and react, try to feel or punch or push, but they lose their power. In the light, our hands are guided by understanding. There're enlightened. So, real power is the glove of light."

"I didn't feel powerful," I scoff.

"Ah, no, you wouldn't, because it's invisible. But your caring gives you power; it makes everything better. Use your power."

"I wanted to call you, but my phone was dead."

Peter puts out his hand. "Let me have it. We'll charge it."

I dig into my pocket and place the phone on the table, but then keep my hand over it.

"What's the problem?" Peter asks. "Ah...you're afraid they'll find you. But Pablo, you're not seeing the other side of this. Your dad will understand. And so's you know, I told them the truth: that you and your dad were with me, fishing, but I couldn't prove it. I wish I'd taken photos."

"Your phone's still in the RIB, charged and waterproofed. It's under the deck. I let air out. Like you showed us—so I could pull it closer to the bank. To hide it."

"Oh, thank God. As long as it's still tied up, your dad has an alibi. His rods and tacklebox will prove you and he were with me. You did the right thing. In the meantime, *I'm* suspect too—I didn't know at the time that you'd hidden it under the deck."

"So why didn't they take Dad and you away in that cop car? My dad is probably in jail and you're here, at home."

"Because, your dad is Latino, like the other men at the mill making those pills. Your dad was caught up in what they call racial profiling. They should have treated him like they treated me. And, that's not all—I know the cop who cuffed us. He'd helped me get someone arrested who was stealing sunflowers from my stand. So, I have the advantage of being known in the community. It's not right that I get preferential treatment, but that's how the system works. You understand?"

"Yes. What I understand is that the system is not fair."

"No, it's not. And your dad is a good man. When we were told we had to come out, he noticed the rope going down through the drop door. It was tied around that person's neck. He was calling for help. Your dad pulled him up and cut the ties that bound his hands. Cut off the rope around his neck. When we left him, he was still groaning on the floor of the mill, but they were about to start shooting. There was no time left; we had to go.

"And now *we* have to go because your mother will be worried. I'll drive you home. We can charge your phone in my truck. We'll put your phone in airplane mode; that way they can't find you, but you can listen to your messages when you want to."

"But...are you sure about this?" I ask.

"You can't run away from problems, Pablo. And the longer it takes to find you, the more suspicious you'll look. And you can't stay with me—I don't even know your mom. So, I must take you home now. Here, call your mother." He holds out the cordless house phone.

I dial. "Mom, it's me."

"Pablo! *Mi querido niño*, where have you been? The police are looking for you. Your father is in jail."

"I know. The man who took us out fishing is bringing me home. I'll tell you everything."

"Hurry," she says.

"Let's go. Come, Pablo," Peter says.

15

OVERDOSE

MINDY

IT'S A QUIET SATURDAY EVENING AT THE MACKAY HOME. AFTER A crazy day the calm feels good. Mom and I go upstairs to freshen up and change. I throw the yoga book onto my bed and empty my pockets, including the capsule, one half light brown, the other half green, into my bedside drawer.

Dad never mentioned it was missing, so maybe I did help him, or perhaps he blamed Mom for taking it. Was that why they argued?

Downstairs, we meet in the kitchen. Mom is at the kitchen counter placing slices on plates and tossing a salad.

"Min, take the pizza out to the deck, would you? We'll eat out there. I'll bring drinks and salad. You want lemonade, right?"

"Yes please."

A warm September breeze is fanning the deck. "Excellent," Dad says. "Smells great." He folds his paper napkin over his leg.

I take a seat facing the dark garden and perfect lawn. Beyond the string of white lights he put up over the railing I see the path of square flagstones leading to the big oak tree. Mom knows I like lemonade because we sip it and chat there after school.

"This is the life, isn't it, Mindy?" Dad says. "How lucky we are, with our home and—oh, excuse me." He holds his phone to his ear. It's permanently on vibrate. "Yes, just a moment." He looks at me. "Sorry Mindy. I have to take this." He walks through the sliding doors just as Mom is coming out with the drinks. "I need a minute," he says.

"Lucas, you need to be with us," she snaps.

"Be right there."

"Yum," I say, to cheer up Mom as she pushes his frozen beer glass in front of his empty table setting.

She hands me my glass of lemonade with clinking ice and sits down with a sigh; her hope for a nice evening has faded. A heaviness comes over me. I think it was spring when we last chatted and laughed—the three of us, a family. Mom raises her eyebrows and bites into the cheese.

"Is he working again?" I ask.

"No. That's Aunt Beth calling. I don't think you know their story."

"No."

"Well," she says, spearing her salad with her fork, "it's taken twenty-one years for them to be friends again."

"Why? What happened?"

"When 9/11 hit, everyone thought she was dead because she worked for a Wall Street accounting firm. But she was on a farm fifty miles from Springfield in nowhere-ville getting clean in rehab, trying to drop a nasty drug habit. Later, when she and Dad reconnected, she said she'd made the decision to leave after she and Dad argued about her habit. They were close, growing up." She tears off a cheesy crust and chews. "Because the flights were delayed, he didn't know where she was until two weeks after 9/11 when the building supervisor let him into her apartment. That's when he found her note.

"He took care of all her bills and contracts. She just abandoned it all. She promised to pay him back. He moved to New York and stayed in her apartment. That was the first year of his residency in the ER at Presbyterian Hospital. One weekend he took a drive out to Montauk. I met him there at an outside bar overlooking the water where he was getting drunk. I was volunteering with the marine program there. And the rest, my dear, is history."

"Wow. Did she get better? Did she pay him back?"

"Eventually. I think she lives in LA now."

Dad rushes back onto the deck. "Sorry. The second call was the hospital. Another case, but it looks like he might make it."

"Dad," I say, "you don't have to excuse yourself when you take those calls. You're doing what you can to help. I'm proud of you."

"Thanks, Min," he says quietly.

"See, Lucas? You don't have to carry that burden by yourself," Mom says. "We're here for you. Now, sit down." She pulls out his chair for him and pats the backrest. "The pizza's good. Drink your beer. Relax. In fact, tell us about your day. It's been terribly hard on you."

He sits heavily. I guess he doesn't want to tell us all the horrible things he saw. And I don't want to hear them. Except, I'm itching to know who, how, why?

"Mindy, is there something specific you want to know?" he asks. "Well, it's just so wrong that someone like Troy Gillis dies of an overdose."

"Yes, it's a terrible shame." Dad says.

"Yeah. Terrible that it's gone viral. But none of the PopJam comments and tweets are about what it actually feels like to OD. What does it feel like?"

What I'm really asking is: does it look like how he acted on

Friday night? How close to death was he? Or do I have this all wrong?

Dad takes a long swig of his beer. "Well, you might be surprised, because the patient looks like they're about to go to sleep. It's not dramatic. At all. In the case of the Gillis boy, he was lying on the floor next to his unslept-in bed. His face was a pallid blue. Calm. His breathing was slow, so we had to get the detox pill into him quickly. Troy's father helped me maneuver his completely limp body into a sitting position, and I tilted his head back, pouring a little water over his tongue and he swallowed the pill."

"I thought the detox was a spray—Narcan, right?" Mom asks.

Dad nods. "Yes, that's what Mrs. Gillis picked up on as well. It's true that police departments, pharmacies, harm reduction centers, even libraries provide free Narcan kits. There are definitely ways for people to get them. But tonight, I preferred to use alternatives because we're seeing contamination; some of the drugs are cut with fentanyl. At least around these parts. So, I use a drug we use for gradual opioid withdrawal and hope for the best. Unfortunately, sometimes we're too late."

Dad bites into a crust.

I think about Troy. How the girls in my class worshipped him, although they were too young for him. They won't believe he was using—he was too great an athlete. But he was injured, so . . . who knows?

"And then? What does it look like when he actually dies?" I ask. I want to know how a living body changes into a dead one.

"Don't be morbid, darling," Mom says. "Come on. Why do you want to know?"

"That's okay," Dad says. "Mindy, it looks like nothing has changed. That's why we monitor the pulse. When it stopped I had the EMT confirm before we declared his death. And, you should know this: the street they live on is just like ours—respectable, middle class. This is why we're—or Mom really—is on your case. We love you and want you to succeed in life."

"We know you will, Min," Mom adds, then smiles and nods her head at me. "You better."

"It can happen to anyone," Dad says. "Anyway, let's go in. We can watch something on Netflix."

"You guys watch," I say. "I'm going to my room—I'm tired."

"You must be," Mom says, "My God, you've been running around all day."

My friend is still out there somewhere. He's not running around; but he is running.

〜

I'M SO EXCITED TO GET SOME SLEEP THAT I DIVE ONTO MY BED; onto the yoga paperback. It looks dated and useless. What was I thinking? Dad will never try yoga. And right now, I'm pretty unexcited about it myself. I flip the pages. The photos of Asian men with man-buns don't move me. I toss the book into the wastepaper bin and check my phone.

Nothing from Pablo.

As I'm drifting off, I hear Mom and Dad walking past my bedroom door.

"It's the question this community is ignoring, Penny," Dad is saying, but I miss the part where he says what the question is.

I put my ear on the door and listen. Mom is saying something about gangs. " . . . they do nothing about them. They're boys and girls just like our kids, but they're slipping narcotics into backpacks and gym bags. The kids are being corrupted—"

"Poisoned," Dad corrects. "Troy's parents will never know that he made the ultimate sacrifice."

"That's right," Mom says.

"Troy sent a message to the lowlifes peddling poisons to our kids," Dad says. "The gangs just lost another customer, who thought he could take the control drugs—Suboxone, or methadone or buprenorphine for the rest of his life. His safety net was gone because even the detox they sell on the street is poisoned."

There's no comfort in this information. If it's true, and he knew it, why did he force Troy to take another pill? But this is not the first time I've jumped to the wrong conclusion because of my snooping.

"Let's hope this scheme works and the drug pushing days are over," Dad is saying. "It's not as if Troy was going to make it—the autopsy will show that the fentanyl in the opioid killed him. But it won't show that it was also in the withdrawal antidote."

"You'll report that, right Lucas?"

"Yes, I will," he says.

Their conversation becomes garbled.

Though I'm desperately tired, my mind won't stop trying to process what I think I just heard. Dad thinks Troy died to make a point, to make a sacrifice to stop the gangs. But he didn't; I don't agree with Dad. Troy died peacefully after a violent battle with addiction.

Dad *must* file that report.

And now, I'm wide awake and they're asleep. Maybe I'll watch a movie downstairs, with my earphones in so I don't wake them.

I leave the lights off in the impeccably clean kitchen, its silky countertops gleaming, lit only by the blue and red glow of appliances. Sipping a glass of water, I see the sleeping garden outside, lit by a moon hiding behind the low clouds sliding silently by, inviting me out. I slip through the den door and pad down the quiet path to the treehouse.

Though I haven't climbed it recently, the weathered ladder up to my little room in the branches is still firm.

Dad and I built the treehouse together. Every Saturday, Dad would be there, drilling, screwing each step, adding planks and beams—me positioning the next one, then watching it go up, around, up into, between the tree's strong limbs. And breathing the woodsy smell of fresh sawdust and mowed lawn. I can't remember if I climbed up there this past summer, but I outgrew it. Those times in the garden are over. Saturdays now have become all about soccer, which I missed today.

From my perch up here I see the world from a distance, separated from its expectations and complications. Our house across the lawn is dark except for an upstairs window. A movement catches my eye—it's Mom, silhouetted, sitting at her sewing table, her head in her hands, shaking. Is she crying?

I'm suddenly short of breath and my heart pounds. I want to run to her and smother her in kisses, but I don't because I'm safe here and I'm afraid if I go to her, I'll find out an awful truth. Mom's been looking after Dad so we can continue to live in our beautiful, lonely house. She's been hiding his disgraceful secret— he doesn't want to get better, which is why he's built a tower of intelligent excuses that only Mom can topple. And maybe me. Can he please, please heal? Because he is my father, the man with whom Mom fell in love, the doctor. He's her only hope for a normal life. Why can't she help him?

I scramble down the ladder and take long springing leaps over the lawn, lean on the sliding door and slip through the kitchen quietly then bound up the stairs and into the sewing room. I don't wait for her reaction. In the split second before I touch her shoulder, she wipes a tear off her face. Our hands collide and veer away.

"Mom. I—"

"Oh, Mindy."

We embrace.

"Is it Dad? Is he okay?"

She shoots a stern look into my eyes. The pitifulness has gone and she's clear-eyed. "He's asleep now, but he's not well. This healing period is hard. I long for us all to be a family again."

I hug her and she surrenders to me, but there's a wall between me and her heart. I know healing is hard, but she won't let herself tell me why.

Her phone rings. "Hello?" She raises her hand to her forehead and squeezes her eyes tight shut. "Yes, yes, of course. I'll leave now." She disconnects and looks at me. "John and Nancy, our friends, have lost their son. Opioids. I must be with them."

"Oh no. I'm so sorry. Yes, you should go," I say.

I didn't know their son, but I knew he'd almost drowned in their swimming pool a few years ago. As she stumbles toward the door of the little sewing room, I look at my phone, squirming with notifications. I read the online headline from our town paper: *FIVE DEATHS FROM OPIODS*. "Mom, look at this." I hand her my phone.

She reads the scant details of the breaking news. "So horrible," she whimpers.

"Dad is helping. He's saving the other druggies who haven't died."

"Yes." Mom is studying my face with her bloodshot eyes. Her nose is running.

"Mom, we're safe because of him. He's a doctor."

But underneath my statement lies the unsettling question of

what he might have done. Or is it only my imagination making him complicit?

"I'm worried, Min. Yes, he can help with the overdoses, but there're so many. He's sedated now; let him sleep. I told him he can call you if he needs you."

16

SACRED HOPE

PABLO

THERE'S A SLIGHT CHILL TO THE AIR AS PETER DRIVES ME HOME with the windows down. These last weeks of summer have started to feel like an early fall. As we weave through the trailer park, I smell carnitas on grills, sweet corn tortillas pressed in iron skillet *comals*. It's the smell of home. Saturday nights are busy. Our neighbors are outside when Peter pulls the handbrake and cuts the engine.

Mom approaches in jeans, her hair tied back in a ponytail. Her cheeks are still flushed from her marathon training run. "Pablo!" She almost shouts my name.

I bail out of the cab and run to her. We hug.

"You okay?"

"Yes."

"Are you hurt?" She presses my arm.

"No."

"Hungry?"

I shake my head. "No. I ate at Peter's house."

Peter steps closer. "Hello, Mrs. Cruz. I'm Peter King. Pablo came to my house. I thought it best to bring him home."

"So glad you did, thank you. Will you come in, Mr. King? We should talk."

"Sure," he says. "Please call me Peter."

In our mobile home kitchen, he asks, "Have you heard from Frederico?"

"He called me from the county courthouse. I've been in contact with an ACLU lawyer through our church. He said if Fred is not part of the drug ring, it'll be easier for them to make a case."

"No kidding," Peter says sourly.

"So, Fred told me he was arrested at the mill on the inlet, which is now a drug drop-off. So why *did* you go there?" Mom asks Peter.

"I wanted to pay my respects. It was selfish. I wanted to look inside and thought it was okay because there was no one around. I was wrong. I'm sorry, Mrs. Cruz. I put your family in danger."

It's bothering me that Peter is taking the blame. I could have said something. Mindy and I knew there were *vatos* below because we saw them last night from the top of the bluff. If I had spoken up then, Dad would not have been arrested.

"I did not want to forget the old mill," Peter says as an afterthought.

I look down. "Dad and I were going to call you after your training run."

"Well, that didn't happen, did it?" Mom says, patting my shoulder. Her laptop on the kitchen table is surrounded with notes and printouts. She's been busy researching Dad's options online—our options. Gathering facts and doing research is how she solves problems.

"Mom, Peter's brother died there," I say.

"Oh . . . I'm sorry, Peter," she says. "But you haven't answered my question: why did you go there? Because they're going to ask you."

"Right. I thought I'd just take a quick look, since we had access from the water. I'm grateful Pablo persuaded me to take the boat out, but I never thought it would turn out this way."

Her hand flap dismisses his apology. "They love fishing. Don't worry about it."

"And . . . I would like Pablo and his father to have my boat," Peter says.

"What do you mean? Why?" Mom asks.

"Why not? I'm too old to go out alone and I want it to go to a family that needs it."

"And? What am I missing?"

"There's no catch. It's yours. Free."

"That's generous. Thank you," Mom says. "But we have to find it first, right? And that might not happen."

"Why not?" Peter asks.

"What if the cops show up tonight and want to question me? They'll see Pablo has come home and we'll have no proof that he and his dad were fishing with you. Fred is already suspected of being part of that drug gang—he'll be deported, or worse. So, Peter, giving us the boat is nice, but right now there's something you can do for us that will be far more helpful. Putting us up for the night will buy us some time. What do you say?"

Peter nods. He's weighing Mom's idea. He must know he'll be breaking the law.

"I'm wanted by the police," I remind him.

"Who's going to know, Pablo? I think your mom is right," he says. "And I want to help. Yes. Stay over at my place—by all means. You can't stay here."

I know we can stay in the obvious places—with relatives,

friends, friends of friends—doing that will put them in danger. Peter's place is a good option. They've already questioned him.

"Then, if you're at my house we can go directly to look for my boat at five tomorrow morning."

"Why wait?" Mom asks.

"So, the tide's rising right now and will be low again just before five, which will be the earliest we can get under the deck to see if it's still there," Peter says. "When Detective Rennecker was questioning me, she mentioned that they'd return for a more thorough search for evidence in the morning after the mill was safe from the remains of the fire. But we can get there before them. In the meantime, the mill is barricaded off by police tape. The detective never said they'd looked under the deck. So we still have a chance."

Mom fixes her dark eyes on Peter. "Let's hope that's true. Okay, Pablo, go pack a bag of clean clothes," she says, "like what you'll wear tomorrow at mass."

THE ROUTE BACK TO PETER'S PLACE IS BLOCKED BY EMERGENCY vehicles. Peter shakes his head as he negotiates around them. I am sandwiched between Peter and Mom.

She leans forward to make eye contact with Peter. "Thank you for doing this, Peter. And by the way my name is Maria."

"It's not Maria," I blurt.

For the first time tonight I see her face soften into a half smile. "Okay, my family first name is Sanchia."

"Yeah? What does that mean?" Peter asks.

"Mom," I say, "tell him all your names."

"Sanchia Esperanza y Tlaxcala. There. Happy?" she says to me.

"*Esperanza* means hope, Peter," I say.

"That's right," Mom says. "And before you ask, Peter, *sanchia* means sacred to me. So that's what I go by—sacred hope," she says. "It's a reminder to me; when hope is sacred, it's not just a dream."

"Ah, I see," he says. "The dream is sacred because it has a purpose. You make it work for you."

"Yes. For a better life," she says.

"I could use some of that *sanchia esperanza* myself," he says. "Everyone could."

An ambulance siren wails in the night. But with Peter's, Mindy's and my one-hundred-and-four years of experience we can solve these problems. The ambulance I heard rushes past us, sowing its frantic lights like seeds of hope.

17

SLEEP OVER

MINDY

PABLO'S TEXT, *YOU THERE?* PULLS ME OUT OF A DEPRESSING place.

After Mom rushed out to be with the grieving family, I made the worst mistake by scanning through the viral online news. I have to talk to Pablo.

His phone rings for a bit, then I hear, "Can't talk, meet me where the JIM suit was."

This is Pablo's code in case the phone is being traced. Of course—Peter's place. Why there? Peter must be hiding him and that's not a good idea because I saw him get arrested with Pablo's dad. So, won't they check to see if Pablo is with Peter?

"No," I say. "Ask Peter to stop by here. I'll be at the bus stop. Don't go to my house." In the background I recognize the rattle of that glove box door in Peter's truck. Peter's talking to a woman whose voice I don't recognize.

"We'll pick you up," Pablo says.

That's not my plan, but I let it go. "Later," I say, and disconnect.

I grab my backpack, pump my bike tires, put on my helmet,

and speed down the drive. It feels good to be out where I don't have to listen to the house. I've checked on Dad several times. His breathing is steady and his sleep is deep. Except for the sirens coming over the roofs of our neighbors' houses, the street is eerily quiet.

At the bus stop, I get off my bike and wait behind the bus stop so no one can see me.

~

WHEN PETER'S RED TRUCK PULLS UP TO THE BUS STOP I WHEEL MY bike to the driver side to speak to Peter.

"Good evening, Mindy. Everything okay?" Peter says.

"Hello, Peter." He looks weary. Maybe he's having second thoughts about the trouble Pablo and I have gotten him into. Pablo and I wave at each other. He's sitting next to his mother, I think.

She smiles at me. "Hello, Mindy. I'm Sanchia, Pablo's Mom. I've heard a lot about you." She seems pretty cool with the pony tail and athlete's build. I can tell where Pablo gets his sports chops. It's a good thing another adult is here—Mom will back off and stop suspecting that Peter is a perv. I have to remind myself that I have a plan. As Dad always says: A good plan today is better than a perfect plan tomorrow. He stole that from Andy Weir, an author I've never read, but I get the point. "Peter," I say. "Maybe I'm wrong, but it looks like you're helping Pablo evade the law, right?"

"For now, yes," Sanchia says.

"In that case, Pablo should stay over at my place," I say. "I can hide him better."

Sanchia shoots a questioning look at Peter. "It's true. They might still want to talk to you. You were with Fred. We could come back to get Pablo when it gets light."

"And you trust him with this family? You don't even know them," Peter says.

Sanchia stares through the windshield. "Look at this neighborhood. I mean, really? He'll be fine."

"That's not the plan, Sanchia," Peter says.

She leans forward, ignores Peter, and asks me, "Mindy, where are your mom and dad?"

"My mom is with friends whose son overdosed tonight, but my dad's home sleeping. He won't know Pablo's with me."

Peter nods slowly, coming around to see Sanchia's point; he's decided not to argue with her—I wouldn't either. "All right, I'll drop you guys off."

"No, people will see your truck," I say. "Our neighbors watch the street. That's why I'm here at the bus stop. Come on, Pablo. Let's go. You can ride on the seat."

There's not a lot of time. I need to get him settled in before Dad wakes up.

Until now, nothing about tonight has felt right, and things have been going downhill fast. But Pablo with me in the house with Mom gone and Dad asleep (or, if he wakes up, crazed), seems right.

I have so many questions for Pablo: what happened while I was at the Op Shop and why was he at the mill? But mostly, I'm enjoying his company with his hands firmly gripping my shoulders while I stand and pedal.

18

NO MORE

MINDY

WHEN I PUNCH IN THE CODE AND THE GARAGE DOOR ROLLS UP, I am faced with an empty garage. Dad has left. If he was sedated, as Mom said, I hope he can drive. I know she's spending the night at her friend's place, and I do feel badly for her. But Dad, out again? I hope he can help, but I also don't—because tonight could end in death. Even his own.

"They're not here, Pablo. You're safe. Let's go up to my room to make a plan," I say.

"You sure about this?"

"Absolutely," I say, knowing absolutes are relative; right now, I'm sure this is relative to what could happen over the next few hours.

In my bedroom Pablo looks at my gray walls with white trim and white plantation shutters that Dad installed for me. My bed is a queen and really comfortable. The thick pile carpet is sage green. The surfaces are spotless, which is what I like. He's stunned.

"I know, it's a great bedroom," I brag.

"Oh yeah . . . It must be hard to survive in here," he says, taking off his backpack.

I point at it as he drops it on my spotless carpet. "What's in there?"

"Clothes. For Mass, tomorrow."

"You mean today."

He looks at my bedside table clock. "Yes." His eyes linger on my drawer. He's looking at the empty pill casing. "What's that for?" he asks.

"My dad."

He swings around to face me. "Mindy, the colors are the same as the pills I saw at the mill."

"Really? Okay, lots of pills have these colors, don't they? Don't worry, I'm not going to take it. I just don't want *him* to. I'm scared. People are dying." I catch a whiff of him. "Hey, you know what? You stink. Time for a shower, my friend."

"I don't stink, but I do smell from the water under the deck, from sweating while I was stuck in the tunnel and from chemical smoke when the mill burned down. I'd love to take a shower."

"Come on then. Bring your backpack. Where's your phone?"

"Ah," he says and hits his forehead. "I left it in Peter's truck. Charging."

"Well, come on, you'll get it when they pick you up in the morning. Wear your Sunday clothes, then you can tell me what happened."

He's even more stunned at my en suite bathroom.

"Enough with the gaping, Pablo. Hurry. Get clean." I point at him. "And don't use my toothbrush. There's a new one in the cabinet."

I close the door.

I can hide him better—that's what I said to Peter and Sanchia. But can I? Outside my window, the moon has moved away, leaving

89

the garden dark. The treehouse is invisible. Good. That'll work if Pablo needs to disappear.

A rumble from downstairs makes my heart thump so hard I can hear it. The sound of the garage door closing is followed by the opening of the kitchen door. It's Dad.

I rush downstairs. Why wouldn't I? I catch him drinking water at the refrigerator. "Dad. Back already? I've been worried about you."

"Hello, Mindy. Yes, I'm back. I was too late to save that patient." He comes over to me to peck my forehead. "This is very worrying. Why are you still up?"

"Homework," I lie.

He takes a deep breath in and lets it out slowly. Before sitting at the kitchen counter, he hitches his chinos up slightly so he doesn't break the crease at the knees. His white open-neck shirt is starched and he wears a red cashmere sweater with the arms tied around his shoulders—he's a Brooks Brothers ad. He motions for me to sit with him. "Have you heard from Mom?" he asks.

"No. Have you?"

He shakes his head. "She's not making or taking calls—I guess that would be insensitive."

"Of course," I say.

I sit with him hoping Pablo has enough time to finish his shower. He's safe for now; Dad never comes into my bedroom. "What's going on?" I ask Dad. "Why are so many people dying on the same night?"

"In one word: fentanyl. It's a synthetic opioid—a painkiller. It's cheap, much more powerful than heroine, and very dangerous. When too much is taken, it's fatal and causes most of the overdose deaths in this country."

"But why now, Dad?"

90

"Because legitimate painkillers are being cut with fentanyl. The counterfeit pills are shaped and colored to resemble Oxycodone pills, which I prescribe to help people manage their pain. Those drugs save lives, but now the gangs have mimicked them. And, as if that's not bad enough, the addicts are now using both coke and opioids. They're called speedballers. What makes it worse is that addicts are chipping now."

"Chipping?"

"Chippers are addicts who take just enough painkillers or opioids or heroin to get high, and then they take an antidote pill— they call them maintenance drugs—which stops them going too far, so they can do it again. And again. Well, now those chippers are chipping with fentanyl, and it kills them. They no longer have drugs to save them. Their safety net is gone. That's what's going on. Sometimes we can bring them back with drugs—that's what I've been doing tonight, training EMTs on how to use alternative detox drugs. So, the drug problem is not all of a sudden, but now it's impossible to control with fentanyl flooding the black market."

So, was the pill I took from him an opioid painkiller, or a legal antidote? Was that pill in his bathroom there just in case he took too many pills for his own pain? And what if that pill is cut with fentanyl?

"But Dad, aren't you afraid? You've been taking pain pills forever . . . how many weeks has it been since your accident?"

He looks tired—it's been a terrible twenty-four hours for him. Yet, he's patient with me. I know he loves me, but this crisis has robbed him of his feelings. "I'm a doctor, Mindy. I can handle it."

"So wait, you *are* addicted?"

"No, I'm saying I'm on painkillers. I'm managing my pain while I heal."

"But you said you can handle it, which doesn't sound good.

Your arm is not in the sling, so can you stop? What does your doctor say?"

"I am my doctor," he says. "And you are right in one respect, Mindy. Stopping is going to be hard, of course."

"Why?"

"Because I'll get sick. It's called dope sickness. It's very hard to cut out something that the body has become tolerant of. These drugs take over the reward center of the brain. So now isn't a good time. I'm needed because of this crisis. Now, I need to get some sleep, young lady. And so do you. Don't worry about me."

I watch him go up the stairs—Mr. Right, the guy who has it all under control.

Halfway up he turns back to me. "Mindy, I'm going to assume I can trust you with the conversation we just had. The information about me is between us. No one else needs to know."

"Don't worry about me," I say, repeating his line with a thumbs-up.

Thing is, he won't worry about me. He'll be too afraid of dope sickness, like it's worse than death.

He smiles and goes upstairs—eager to get into his bedroom so he can go into that state I saw him in on Friday night—that other scary world, leaving me here at the counter, staring at the powder-blue toaster, paralyzed because I'm out of ideas. He talks about those other people losing their safety net, but he doesn't see me free falling through *my* safety net here at home.

I'm unable to head Dad off from finding Pablo up there in my bathroom. I can't help thinking how alone he must feel right now. And here I sit, as if I don't care if he's discovered. Suddenly it seems like everyone trusts me to keep their secret. The problem is, with each secret I feel heavier, more shut down, slower.

So, Dad thinks it's okay to carry on this way. He assumes me and Mom will take care of him through his dope sickness—but just not now, because we're less important than his patients. And because now isn't a good time, he'll go on using. It'll never be a good time for him. Either way, whether he's using painkillers or he's dopesick, he's not my dad any more than he's still Mom's husband—that's why she goes to her sewing room to cry; she's trapped. She's playing a double game protecting dad from the same thing as those other people are dying from.

If Pablo is right, I may already have saved Dad's life by stealing that pill. But what about the next one? Did he get more when he was out? If I could stop him using, would I get him back? Probably, and I don't even care how sick he gets.

Mom and I *will* take care of him. I'll take his drugs away. Because there's never a good time, the time has come. I must act . . . now.

This is my real plan, I realize: there can be no more drugs for Dad.

This is the real reason I wanted Pablo here with me—though hiding him is good too. Later, when this is all over Mom and I will find a doctor for Dad.

He's probably swallowing a pill right now, or planning to. I quietly rush into my bedroom and close the door. Pablo's dressed in his nice clothes. It's the first time I've seen him with his hair brushed.

"My dad's home," I say.

"Oh, man! Now what?"

"I need your help." I point at the pill casing. "If he has more of these, I think he'll take one now. We need to stop him."

"We?"

"Yes, you and I. We'll tell my dad to take you home, but you'll tell him to drop you at Peter's place where your mom is."

"When he tells your mom she'll call the police," Pablo says. He looks at me in that seriously incredulous way when I push him beyond the realms of possibility.

"He won't talk to Mom before we leave, because my dad said she wasn't returning calls. She thinks he's still asleep and won't want to wake him. Listen, Pablo, you're my friend. I need you to do this for me. Return the favor I did for you at the pit. He doesn't know about you, or your dad, or the mill." Dad won't call 911 because he doesn't want them too close to his—our—secret, and he definitely doesn't want someone else's kid in his home. So, he'll drive you home, for sure.

"Why would your dad think we live in a house like Peter's?" Pablo asks.

"Why not? If your family was legal and your game was successful you could easily afford Peter's house. Come on. We'll do this together. Don't worry. He's not violent. You can help me save him."

He nods. "You better be right."

I hand him my phone. "Here. Call your mom."

His fingers stab my phone and he stares at me while it rings. And rings. "She's not picking up."

"Let's go, Pablo." I have no idea if this is going to work. Pablo looks scared, which is the perfect face for Dad to see. As we leave my bedroom, I see the pill in my drawer and decide it's best to take it with me. I wrap it in a tissue and shove it into my pocket.

My palms are sweating as we approach Dad's door. I knock. Silence. Am I too late?

"Hey, Dad," I call in a loud whiny voice. "Will you take my friend home? Please?"

The door swings open. He's standing at the foot of the bed with his mobile to his ear, saying something or giving advice. I recognize that tone. He's wired. Good. It's like that with him; either way up or way down. He eyes us as he speaks, then says, "Okay any time," and pockets his phone.

"Sorry, Dad," I say. And I mean it. "This is Pablo. His mother couldn't pick him up because of the ambulances."

"Oh, you didn't say you had a friend over. Hello, Pablo. *¿Cómo estás?*"

Pablo looks down like he's being scolded, then, still not saying anything, he looks up at Dad with a toothy, defiant smile and shoots out a thumb-up.

"There you go. *Bueno.* Well, let's get you home," Dad says, wiping the white powder from his nostrils with the back of his hand.

MONEY TO BURN

MINDY

DAD KNOCKS ON PETER'S FRONT DOOR. STANDING HERE, PABLO and I are chilled by the black September night.

Sanchia opens the door. "Pablo! Mindy!" she shrieks. "Oh, hi. I'm Pablo's mom," she says to Dad, calming down. She's clearly confused by Dad's intimidating presence and bravely sticks out her hand. He's much taller than her, so she looks like she's going to poke him in the stomach.

"Lucas MacKay. I belong to Mindy," Dad says with a broad smile, though he does not shake her hand. "Just dropping off Pablo."

"Oh . . . thank you," Sanchia says. She steps forward and gently pulls Pablo's inside. "Go ask Peter for some chocolate milk." She's smart. She wants to get Pablo out of the way. She knows something's wrong—this is not the plan. From her point of view, I have blown Pablo's cover. The fact that I have a father on the edge will not be her concern.

Dad scratches the back of his neck and rubs his forearms. He's craving his next pill. I can't break the promise I made to him—to keep his addiction between him and me, but I must also follow my No-Drugs-For-Dad plan.

It's now or never, or I lose control. "Dad, I need to use the bathroom."

"Really Min?" he says, ushering me into the house.

"Well, come inside," Sanchia says. We follow her, weaving through the living room boxes. Normally, I'd be chatting away, but I don't say anything in case I say something I shouldn't.

Peter is slouched at the kitchen table groggily sipping coffee. Opposite him a laptop is open with papers scattered around it; it hasn't taken Sanchia long to settle in. He pushes himself away from the table and straightens when we enter.

"Good morning to you, Doctor." Peter extends his hand to Dad.

"Nice to finally meet you, Mr. King." Dad shakes Peter's hand.

"You know my name."

"I know your sunflowers."

"Well, there you have it. Coffee?"

I start hopping, like I'm going to burst. "Bathroom?"

"Oh. Here. Follow me," Peter says.

At the bathroom door, I say, "Peter, my dad's on pain pills. Can you stop him from taking more? I'm scared for my safety driving me home if he takes another one."

"What are you talking about?" Peter asks.

I don't blame him for being confused. There's no time to explain about Dad's accident. His big excuse.

"I don't need to use the bathroom, okay? I just *don't want him to take anything now*, okay? Can you keep him busy?"

"Okay, Mindy. I understand. I'll see what I can do."

He points at the bathroom door. "Go in here for a minute or two."

I go into the bathroom and listen. On the other side of the door, I hear Peter talking in a low voice. He's on his phone.

"Detective . . . it's Peter King. I think you should come over . . . my place . . . well, okay . . . you're watching it? Just come now."

I hear his footsteps going down the hall. There—it seems he *is* going to help me. I count to twenty as I run water over my hands.

When I return to the kitchen, Peter, Dad and Pablo are sipping coffee, not talking to each other.

"Well, we should get going, Mindy," Dad says.

"Thank you for dropping him off, Doctor." Sanchia says. "Have you been on call because of the opioid deaths?"

I wonder at this question. Why would Sanchia start that conversation now?

"Yes. I guess the word is out," Dad says. "Terrible about those families."

Sanchia nods. "So sad—but are their families actually surprised when they eventually overdose?"

Dad has been rubbing his itchy face. He pulls his hands away and stares wide-eyed at Sanchia. "Yes. The addict's mindset, and those around them, is denial. And then one day it's too late."

Sanchia faces Dad, "So, they choose not to stop. And their loved ones are okay with that?" She shifts her shoulders square-on and crosses her arms. "They have money to burn. What do you see when you make the rounds? Hungry families? Kids without clothes?"

"No." Dad shakes his head, biting his tongue. "But addiction can lead to that."

"Yeah, maybe. Eventually," Sanchia says. "In the meantime, they want to get high. They only care about themselves."

Dad turns his back on Sanchia. He does not want to hear anything more from her. He's irritated because she has just described him, and he's heard enough. "Ready, Mindy?" He turns back to Peter. "By the way, Mr. King, what about you? What's going on here?"

"I don't have to explain anything to you, Doctor. On this night when so many people have died, I'm helping Pablo's family. I understand you're trying to connect the dots, but, respectfully, it's none of your business."

Peter has no idea what Dad does and does not know. But he's not going to be bullied.

Pablo and I have turned Peter's life downside-up and set him on a new path. In return, he knows what he wants: to get Pablo's dad back. I wish he could do the same for me. I know he understands because his brother died from contaminated alcohol. Tonight has turned into a perfect storm: two families in trouble, people overdosing, and an old man getting ready to live his remaining days in a depressing apartment. I need a plan to make our world whole again.

And Peter's right—the secret between the three of us is no one else's business. But I'll give him an answer.

"Dad, we don't know what's going on. Especially not tonight. It's like you're asking, 'Why do we exist on this planet?'"

"Mindy, don't be silly. It's time you got some sleep, young lady."

"Really?" I whine.

Dad is scratching his forearms again, like he has mosquito bites. "Come, come, Mindy let's get you home."

I follow Dad out the house and turn to see Pablo give me a little wave—as if to say, *I hope you're okay.* Dad's forehead is sweating. Where is that detective?

Dad swerves as he backs down the drive. I can't stop his craving any more than he can, and now I think I might die in this car tonight. Either he gets help or he takes that detox pill, which will tide him over for the next six hours, just in time to get high after breakfast tomorrow morning. Unless it doesn't kill him first.

But I won't be home. I'll be on the school soccer field. With no one around I'll practice my penalty kicks.

20

THE DYI LIFE

PABLO

WHEN I RETURN TO PETER'S KITCHEN FROM THE BATHROOM, flashing strobe lights spray red and blue onto the walls. The three of us run to peer through the living room sheers. A siren whoops. Tires screech.

"Where can we hide?" Mom asks Peter.

"Go into the sunflower field at the back." He points down the passage to an exterior Dutch door with windows in the upper half. "But wait. Look at this."

The street is blockaded with police vehicles as far as I can see into the night.

"Sanchia, they're not coming for you guys," Peter says. "The activity appears to be next door." A patrol car is blocking a black BMW, preventing it from leaving.

I point. "That's the car Mindy's dad drives."

Mom holds my shoulder as she leans closer to the window, spellbound.

"They're arresting him," Peter says.

"Oh no, they're taking Mindy away too," Mom says.

It's not going well for them. I feel so bad for Mindy as she watches her dad being frisked, his hands planted on the hood of his car. An officer pries the trunk open. He reaches into a plastic carry bag and pulls out several small white boxes.

"Mindy'll be all right, Pablo," Peter says, patting my shoulder. The doctor and Mindy are led to separate state trooper cruisers. They pull away, weaving through the mayhem of other departing vehicles.

Peter sighs. "Well, it looks like you're both spending the night here. I'll get you squared away. I'm going to make cocoa. Want some?"

Mom nods with a quick smile. "Sounds good, right *peque?*"

Peter is right—it'll be okay, because despite her dad being apprehended by the police, Mindy's been able to keep her dad off drugs, at least for now.

PETER LEAVES MOM AND ME SIPPING COCOA IN THE KITCHEN.

"Pablo," Mom says, "in the morning you and me are going to the police station to find out where your dad is."

"But if I'm not missing, they won't have an excuse to hold him at the police station. They'll hand him over to Immigration. What'll happen to us, Mom?" I protest.

"Stop with this theory of yours. I've heard enough," she says. Now Mom sounds like Peter. He told me the longer it takes them to find me, the more suspicious I look. "Don't worry about that," Mom says. "Focus on you. You have a gift with graphics— designing characters. I need you back with me, man! If we have to leave the US, we can find work on the internet anywhere in the world. Isn't that what we decided? You and I can sell our game online. What did I say we were?"

"Indie creators," I say.

Peter's back from setting up the spare bedroom for Mom and me. "Innovators," he says, waving his forefinger at the ceiling fan.

"Is my phone still in your truck?" I ask.

He glances at a charger in the wall socket attached to my phone.

Mom wags her finger at me. "No. Do not take your phone off airplane mode. You're still wanted by the authorities. You can do it tomorrow."

What will happen to Mindy now? How soon will Mindy's mom come to get her if she's not answering her phone? In the meantime, she'll be held at the police station—and that's not right.

Peter shakes his head at the messy kitchen table. "Sanchia, what *are* you working on?"

I want Mom to share with Peter how she taught herself to code and now has a game that has started to make some money. But she won't share that, or that she publishes and promotes our game herself. She turns to look up at him. "Alright, Peter, check this out. Pablo is the creative talent in this family."

She moves aside so Peter can see the laptop screen of a simulated video game player. "Pretty cool, hah?"

Peter leans closer to the screen. The bright, splashy screen displays our red and black *Para Dize IV* logo, which Mom and I designed.

"That's fun," Peter says. "Is that the game creator?" he says pointing at the title credit *Santiago del Paraiso*, below the logo.

"Sure. There're great," she says.

"They?"

"Yes. They created the characters, wrote the stories, and designed and coded the actions. And did the drawings. You're looking at them."

"I don't follow," says Peter.

Mom beams a wide guilty grin.

Her smile is infectious and Peter bursts out laughing. "You two created this—really?"

"That's us. Let me show you." Mom changes screens too fast for Peter to track, but half the screen is now the home page of the game; the other side is a dense block of code. "Watch this." Her fingers fly across the keys, changing things in the maze of lines. On the adjacent panel Peter sees the game is now credited to *Sanchia and Pablo Cruz*.

Peter shakes his head. "The amazing Santiago team. You've created magic. Who's this character?" he asks, pointing at the laptop. "He looks kind of mean."

"Hey, don't run down Mr. Ke! He inspired this character. Pablo based him on my boss at the laundromat where I iron shirts. See the Red Army Mao cap?"

"So why spend your time ironing shirts when you could be putting everything into this game…Isn't *this* your career?"

"Because he doesn't make me fill out forms; he pays me cash."

"So, he's your front? Your cover for the work you do on the game?" Peter asks. "I ask because I wonder about Pablo. How can he do his homework, help Fred cut down trees, train Mindy with soccer drills, and still do the graphics for the game? It seems too much to ask of a young boy."

"Well, Pablo", Mom says, looking at me. "You can stop at any time, right?"

"I don't want to stop," I say.

Mom turns back to Peter. "It's all part of his education. He likes being challenged, and I don't see that happening in his school. I want him to make the most of his opportunities. Fred and

I do the same because we could lose it tomorrow. My job at the laundromat is not illegal."

"And Fred?"

"He has his own business. There have been cases where an undocumented person owned his own business and it was a point in his favor defending against deportation. But I'm still afraid I might ruin Pablo's chance of becoming a US citizen."

I've never heard Mom say this before.

"I get it," Peter says. "Opportunity doesn't fall from the sky. You make it happen."

"We try. Sometimes it's hard to pay the rent. Our only option to make the life we want."

"And Pablo? How did you learn this computer art?" Peter asks.

"Oh, Mom and I do our Kahn Academy lessons—"

"Which are free, by-the-way," Mom says.

"I learn graphics the way Mom learns to develop games. And when we work, we look up English lessons. Mom comments on my art—she doesn't allow any shooting or murder or war in our game. We compile her code together. If we have to do it again because it's wrong we have to explain why to each other. And we start over—a lot."

Sanchia smiles. "We're keeping the dream alive. My code is in the cloud. Open source. Anyone can use it, or improve it."

"You give it away?" Peter asks.

"Yes," I say. "Mom has thousands of followers."

"They can take my code, but they can't take our vision or the look and feel of the game because that comes from my son," she says and gives me a high five.

"In the meantime, you're living on the edge."

"Kind of. But, if we're busted and have to go to immigration court, they'll see we're honest. But what about you, Peter?"

"What about me?" Peter asks.

"Looks like you're preparing to move out. You gave us your boat. Seems like you're packing it all in," Mom says.

"Well, I'm old. I can't run the farm anymore. I look at you and Pablo and . . . I'll be honest, I'm jealous. You have your whole life ahead of you."

"Hey, Peter? You don't have to let it go. We can run your farm," I say.

"Pablo. That's not for us to decide." Mom says.

Peter stands back and rubs his chin. "You know, that crazy idea just might make sense."

"What are you thinking?" Mom asks. "You keep the house and we run the farm?"

"Something like that. We can divide the profits between us—a partnership. You won't need Kickstarter and you'll have free board and broadband internet twenty-four-seven."

"That works for me," Mom says. "We could manage the social media, the farm stand, and the deliveries. You've seen our skills. Fred can handle the farming and harvesting. We could make this farm work again. Give us one season to prove we can do it."

"We're in sunflower season now," Peter says. "So, it's not too late—if we do it now."

I've been watching this negotiation and realize that my creativity comes from Mom.

She dries the mugs with a dish towel. "First, let's get Fred out of the county jail."

"Right. And to do that we need to prove he was with me, fishing in the sound," Peter says. He takes the towel from Mom and hands me my phone. "Leave the mugs and get some sleep. I'll wake you at five-thirty."

"Okay. Good night."

"Good night—partner," Peter says with a sly smile.

In the spare bedroom Mom says, "Pablo, this could be incredible for us."

"I know," I say. "Did you see his face light up?"

"Oh yes; you just gave him ten years of life—if it works out."

But our dream is broken by the sound of the front door chime.

21

ON THE RUN

PABLO

THE DOOR CHIMED BECAUSE DETECTIVE RENNECKER HAS questions.

"She knows Peter has company," Mom whispers. "She's seen the mugs drying on the rack."

"Mom," I whisper. "Go talk to her. Tell her I'm sleeping and you don't want to wake me."

She stares at me, taking in what I'm asking, then paces up the passage into the kitchen.

With thoughts of our future lives in this house racing through my head, must I now tell the detective what I know—before we have evidence of the boat? The more I think about it, the more thoughtless it seems. Why not delay until we can prove our innocence?

While the adults discuss things, I grab my phone and creep up the passage to the Dutch door. Outside, I see the dark sunflower field through the windows in the upper half of the door. I unlock the latch and side through. I am about to run across the backyard when I catch Detective Rennecker's voice, saying, "I could arrest you right now," she says. "You think you're too old? Think again. You don't have to protect the boy. Where is he?"

"We don't know," I hear Mom say.

This means she's thinking what I'm thinking—delay.

"I'm not going to ask again," the detective says.

"Detective, you saw what the doctor had in his trunk," Mom says.

Something is said, muffled, then I hear Peter's voice. "So how come I got to walk away after the fire, but Fred who was with me gets to ride in the paddy wagon with the other scumbags?"

"I'm not answering your questions. You're answering mine," the detective says. "I'll remind you, this is a sanctuary town . . . we don't arrest illegal aliens. Now, excuse me."

I hear heavy footsteps coming down the passage and run like hell for the sunflowers. I peek through the leaves and briefly catch the three fleeting adults pass the window in the door. I wait.

Mom screams. "Pablo!"

The Dutch door swings open "Pablo!" Mom shouts into the field.

I know she's on my side. She'll agree with me running like this.

"Pablo?" she shouts again into the blackness of the sunflower field.

Detective Rennecker joins Mom in the door. Carried in the wind I hear her question: "Where will he go?"

Mom's calming down, collecting her thoughts as she no doubt ponders the detective's question. "I have no idea."

"I think we need to work through these loose ends at the station house. And I'm sure you want to see your husband. You're coming too, mister King."

Winds gusts ripple in waves across the tipping sunflowers. Her question really is for me—where *will* I go? And the answer is obvious—I need to retrieve the boat, our boat from under the deck. We were going to go there at dawn, but I'll go there now.

There are several ways to the mill: by the dead-end road, by boat, by climbing down the bluff. But the tunnel is the best way—especially if you don't want to be seen.

22

THE STATION HOUSE

MINDY

AFTER DAD IS TAKEN AWAY, OFFICERS DRIVE ME TO THE COUNTY police station. The nice one in the passenger seat twists around. "Don't worry," he says. "We've left a message for your mother. We'll take care of you until she picks you up."

"Why did you arrest my dad?" I ask, though I think I know.

"We didn't arrest him; we just need to talk to him," the officer says.

Mom's not going to be listening to messages so I'll be waiting for a while.

At the station, the booking sergeant ignores me as he checks me in. Inside this ugly building I feel even more invisible. I'm led to an office and told to wait. It smells like bubblegum and perfume. A nameplate says Det. Kristin Rennecker. The desk is piled with stacks of paper, each with a swarm of sticky notes attached. I'm thirsty and their internet sucks, but then my phone vibrates. It's Pablo. "Where are you?" I ask.

"Tunnel. To get my boat. I can't talk, but the dealers have come back to get the pills that weren't burnt in the fire. Mindy, they're the same colors as the one in your bedroom."

"Pablo, you need to get out of there. I'll call you back."

Someone has to hear about these pills. Are they the contaminated antidote pills? My phone vibrates. I've received an email from Pablo. There's a voice recording attached. I open it and hear voices I don't recognize. Evil voices. I pause the recording and rush into a larger office next to this one.

An officer with lots of silver stripes on his shoulders gets out of his chair. "Hello, what can I do for you?" he asks. Then he shouts over me. "Smith, get in here."

On the double, Officer Smith appears at the door. "What's up, Chief?"

Now is my chance. I have made a mistake by barging into the chief's office, but really, the cops need to deal with Pablo. I'll deal with Dad; he's my responsibility. I hold my phone up and play the recording. Both officers step closer and listen. A voice is saying, "No . . . business was fine before . . . before fentanyl . . . but he wants more, the chippers want more, they'll pay anything for it. I can't walk away—he's holding my wife and daughter . . . until it's all on the street—" The voice is drowned in hiss and the recording stops.

The Chief says, "Rennecker, get on this. I want a report every hour."

Smith is on his phone. He stares down at me. "We're going to hold you here a little longer, then someone from CPS will be here to take care of you."

He walks me to a different desk in the open-plan area. I google CPS. Child Protective Services. I don't feel abused, as the text explains, except—really—where are my parents right now? I wish I could run away with Pablo. CPS sounds like they take charge of kids, but the quality-of-service comments on the website have an average of one out of five stars. I'm not available for this.

They've seated me at an open desk where Officer Smith and others can keep an eye on me. I speed-dial Mom again. This time she picks up. My guess is she's so done with grieving for her friend. Is she now ready to find out where her own family is?

"I'm in the car now, honey. Be home soon."

"Mom, I'm at the police station. The cops have taken Dad in for questioning."

"My God...what happened?" She must not have spoken to Dad yet.

"He was stopped in the car and they found pills in his trunk. He'll give you the details. But don't go home—you need to come here."

"Where? Where are you?"

"Here," I say. "Talk to this officer."

I walk over to Smith and hold out my phone to him. "It's my mother."

As Smith gives her directions to the county station, I find myself amazed that Mom has still not said she is sorry for leaving me alone in our house. But can I really blame her? How can she lead me on like the MacKay's are just fine; we're managing the crisis. Is she really that clueless? I have believed their story about Dad's pain, but how can a doctor not manage his own pain? And the system looks the other way. It doesn't see how sick he is—how sick *it* is. Because he *is* the system. A system with an addiction problem. Smith hands me back my phone.

"Mom, you're picking me up first, right?"

"I'm picking Dad up at the jail, Min. We'll swing by the station to get you after that."

"No, Mom, please come here first. They're talking about Child Protective Services. You need to be here to show them I'm not forgotten."

"Oh Min," she sighs. "Stop being dramatic. All right, I'll get you first."

"Mom. . . . Dad should be in the hospital."

I hear the drone of the car in the background. She sniffs. "He's been helping people all night. He's tired. This is all a misunderstanding. But listen, I'm driving. I'll see you soon, hon."

Not soon enough. Officer Smith is talking to a woman dressed in a long skirt with a long cardigan over it. In that outfit she has to be CPS. They're trying to decide what to do with me. I'll call Peter —he'll know what to do. But before that I need to talk to Pablo. His phone goes to message.

MOM HAS ARRIVED, AND THOUGH I HAVEN'T SEEN HER, I HEAR THE raised voice of the officer who checked me in. "You can't go in there, ma'am!"

I hear Mom say, "Just watch me."

I know that voice. The shockwaves ripple through the station house. Officers crane their necks to see who's making a scene. Mom is striding toward me.

"Miss, don't wander off," a young officer warns me.

"My mom's here," I say. I wonder if she's too late. Will CPS give me back to her if they see her in this seemingly manic state? She gets like this when she's afraid. When she sees me, she opens her arms. I hug her waist. I see the nervous cardigan lady and Officer Smith approaching behind her.

"How're you doing, Min?" she asks. She bends to make eye contact and strokes my cheek.

"How's Dad?" I ask.

"Right." Adjusting to an operational mode, she turns to face Officer Smith. "I need you to tell me where my husband is."

"Did you say *I need to?*" Smith asks. His face flushed and he looks ticked off. "We'll find out where he's being held, but you need to stay here until we get your daughter sorted with Child Protective Services."

"I don't think so. You're not going to sort me, okay, Officer?"

From behind me I hear the now familiar voice of the detective. "I got this."

Rennecker has arrived. She's with Sanchia and Peter, who wave at me. My heart rate quickens—do they have news of Pablo?

Mom has noticed Peter and Sanchia. "What is that man doing here? Do you know, Mindy?"

"No, Mom. He didn't check with me. He and I will have to have a little chat."

"Don't get snarky with me," she says under her breath.

The chief approaches. "You must be Mrs. MacKay," he says. "I just met your daughter."

Mom nods her head at him. "Good morning, Officer," she says. Amazing how she suddenly calms down when she has the attention of someone in charge. That's talent.

In the meantime, if Dad takes another pill he could die. I'm tired of the jabbering. I step between Mom and the chief. "Hello, excuse me, I'm here." I raise my hand. "Is my dad okay?" I ask the chief. I look back at Mom. "He couldn't even back down the drive. He needs help."

They look down at me. The room goes quiet.

Mom tilts her head at the chief. "She's frightened."

The chief turns with his phone now at his ear. He nods, keeping an eye on me, then disconnects. "Ma'am," the chief says to Mom. "Your husband is in intensive care."

"My God...why!" Mom asks.

I just told her why, though I didn't know he was at the hospital.

"They'll let you know. I'm not a doctor," the chief says.

"Which hospital is it?" Mom demands.

"I'll take it from here, chief," Rennecker says.

Mom stomps her foot. "I asked where the hell is he?" Mom's finally waking up, the dawn of panic spreading on her face.

The chief steps closer to Mom. "Your husband is at Stonybrook Hospital. He's heavily sedated and under suicide watch. However, you should know he's being guarded by my arresting officer while he's there."

"Why?"

Rennecker is pretty cool—she manages to keep calm while surrounded by this crazy crowd. "We found boxes of opioid antidote in his car, and although he's saving lives with these medications he nevertheless could have committed a crime."

"What? Why?" Mom yells, outraged.

"Because, unfortunately, Mrs. MacKay, there were no prescriptions." Rennecker says.

"That's outrageous," Mom says.

"Perhaps it is," the chief says, "given it is temporarily needed to for emergencies. The CDC is looking into the efficacy of the pills. We've searched the mill since they put out the fire, but we didn't find any evidence of cocaine, heroin or opioids. But we did find opioid antidotes contaminated with fentanyl. We want to know if there's a connection to what your husband had in his car."

"My God." Mom shakes her head and stares blankly at the detective and the chief. "Did you say suicide?"

"They tell me it's a precaution they take because of the depression from withdrawal," the chief says. "You should go.

Please take your daughter with you—so you don't have to leave her with Child Protective Services."

"Before you go," Rennecker says. "I have a question for you, Mindy."

"Now what?" Mom snaps.

"It's really for both Mindy and Mrs. Cruz—about finding Pablo. Why did the owner want that particular tree trimmed?"

"How would she know?" Mom says, agitated. "We *really* need to go."

"She *would* know," Sanchia corrects, "because they're buddies and tell each other everything."

Sanchia gets the stink-eye from Mom.

"Mindy—if you don't mind," says the chief. "Do you want to add anything?"

And I should, because, when I think of it, I made this meeting happen. I hid Pablo at my place and caused all of this. But I shake my head because Peter has his pointy finger out again.

"I live practically next door to that property—I know it. My brother died there in 1969 from twelve-year-old hooch. But they sealed the shaft and fenced it off when the new owner moved in. I can only think, because that tree was a landmark for boaters, trimming it, making it disappear was a signal of some sort," Peter says. "I did meet the owner once. He stopped by to get sunflowers. Introduced himself. Gave me his business card."

Rennecker is curious. "What *is* his business?"

"Hedge fund manager, I think. Last name is Gray. Matthew Gray. Very eager. Nervous type. Said he wants to escape the city for a peaceful place in the country to be with his kids on the weekends."

The chief is nodding, taking it in. "He and the kids . . . no wife? What else do you know about him?"

"Nothing. That was the last time I saw him," Peter says.

Sanchia is scratching at her phone. "Here," she says and holds it out. "Is this him?"

Peter squints. "Looks like him."

"Okay, let's see if there's a connection to the owner," the chief says. "Rennecker, coordinate with FBI White Collar Crime. Let them follow the money. Let's make a deal with mister Cruz. Get him out of lockup."

As this sinks in, I pump my fists at my side. Can Pablo come out of hiding now? I put up my hand. "We're leaving now," I say, like a good schoolgirl, which, I have to remind myself, is what I am supposed to be.

I grab Mom's hand and pull her away, and I don't let go until we're out of that stupid building.

23

DR. BALD

PABLO

I HAVE THE SAME VANTAGE POINT I HAD BEFORE FROM THE TOP OF the water tank in the tower. Through the hole in the roof I see the burned-out timbers and the shell of what was once the old mill. However, the deck is only partly burned, which means the deflated boat should still there. It had better be.

I'd love to reach out to Mom. Let her know I'm safe, and that I ran away to get the proof we need. I'm not trying to be a troublemaker. I'd also like to see how Mindy's doing. When they led her to the police cruiser, she hugged herself like she was freezing cold and looked so lost. But I have to stick to the plan and focus on the goal: getting the boat untied and freed from the deck and the mill. Only then will I be able to contact the police.

A breeze has sprung up since first light, as it always does. I used to watch Dad get ready for work, and every time, with the promise of a new day, the shifting air would transform with the light to become a breeze, picking up strength as the sun broke the skyline over the Fresno farm where we lived. He would return home, windswept and tired, though never without hope at the end of the long day, only to go back the following morning.

The breeze carries a squeak, something metal, swinging in the wind, but all I see is the fanned smoke from the burnt-out timbers. However, the more I listen, I realize the squeaking does not quicken with the increasingly buffeting gusts. Neither is the squeaking quickened by the waves that do not change the timing of the tides. I remember Dad telling me that. He also added that often things are not as they appear. I have to look below the surface, see the currents, see the slope of the seabed. And I should be aware that above me, the moon is invisibly pulling on the ocean's surface, but it's the wind that is making the waves.

Something else is causing the squeak. It's coming from somewhere closer, perhaps beneath what used to be the floorboards of the mill. Most of those boards have burned through. I can see the shifting waters and remember Doctor Bald, whose life I might have saved. Exactly which piling he was hanging on to is hard to tell, yet I think I make out the frame of the drop door that could have committed him to his watery death.

In the lull of the gusts, I hear water rushing under the mill, and —faintly—the grind of something heavy. But nothing moves except the water and the wind.

However, on the mostly burned-out second story, I see Doctor Bald—he's somehow survived. He clambers over the side of a large storage bin, supported by the robust carpentry of the original grist mill, which I assume was used to store wheat.

I watch him step carefully around the timbers and down the barely useable staircase. He loses his footing and slides through the stair treads. But he hooks his elbow around the next step down. Below him, there are no floorboards to break his fall. He'll drop into the fast-moving current of the outgoing tide.

He looks down and I hear him shout, "Oh, no . . . "

It is truly a miracle he's alive. And his miracle might be my opportunity.

I scramble off the water tank and grab a length of rope from the fishing gear in the tower, then run across the road.

"Señor, let me help you."

"Thank you," he pants.

I mount the shaky stairs and shove the rope into the bald man's free hand, then I loop the rope over a higher beam—making a primitive pulley. "Hold the rope," I say.

I run around to help his bare feet find a board to land on. When he lets go, I break his fall with my body so that he ends up on top of me, with the rest of the rope falling onto his head—not what I intended. I push him off, stand and look down at him as he throws the rope off his head. I give him a hand up.

"How's your neck?" I ask.

He points his index finger at me. "You're the kid who helped me."

I nod.

"I thought I was a goner. Why are you here?"

"I'm waiting to get my boat, when the tide changes."

Dr. Bald points his finger up and listens. "You hear that? Come with me. The tidal gate should be opening soon."

That was the squeaking I heard. I'm about to find out what a tidal gate is because he's leading me to the drop door. I can't believe he'd go down there again, but he's lowering himself through it. He beckons me. "Come, I have a job for you."

To the side of the opening there are stone steps that I haven't seen previously. I follow him along a stone parapet and now see what's causing the squeaking.

"When the tide changes, the gate is supposed to swing open, diverting the water over the turbines that grind the wheat," Doctor

Bald says. "But it must be stuck. I want you to go in there and get something for me."

I jerk my chin up in defiance. "No way."

"What do you mean, no?"

"First you help me get my boat, then I help you." I've saved his life—twice. So now it's payback time. I don't care if he's older than me or that he's a doctor. To me, he's just Bald, and that's what I'll call him. He needs to help me get the boat out from under the deck. Even if I'm able to free it I don't think I can work the foot pump by hand without sinking the outboard motor. I need his help. "You're going to help me pull my boat out from under the deck."

"Oh no, you get my package first, then I help you," Bald says.

"I don't trust you. Once you have your package, then what? You going to walk into town in your state? You don't even have shoes on. And you don't want to be seen, so a boat getaway is best for you."

"I suppose you're right. But show me some respect—I'm a doctor of pharmacology, not a gofer for a teenager—no offense. Ah, we're right here. Can't you just slip though and hand me the Ziploc bag? It'll take you two seconds."

I'm not going to respect this doctor of farmer something-or-other who hides stuff behind a tidal gate. But I could hold onto the bag and threaten to throw it into the water unless he helps me.

I lower myself into the cold current and wedge myself through the narrow gap of the gate.

"Good," the doctor says. "Now, there's a plastic bag taped to the dry part next to the hinge. Do you see it?"

"Yes. Okay, let's get my boat."

"Give me the bag."

I jiggle the bag through the gap in the gate, taunting him. "Boat first." The bag contains white boxes of medications. I dangle the bag inches above the water.

"No, no. Don't do that. Okay, we'll get your boat."

I return the bag to where I found it, then slip back though the gap. "Let's go." I grab the rope and lead the way, splashing through the cold shallow water close to the bank, passing below the burned and smoking timbers of what was once the deck. Bald is trying to keep his bare feet dry. "Hurry up, or I'll leave without you," I say.

The crumpled gray neoprene of the deflated boat—Peter's prized RIB that he gave us —is barely visible in the low light. Bald and I don't talk much above the sound of the cold swirling water. I tie the rope to the handle on the boat. We jiggle it free.

"Hold the motor up, while I pump," I tell Bald.

When I open the hatch door to retrieve the pump, I see Peter's phone, powered down and still sealed in the bag. The doctor cannot know about this. I press the foot pump against a pilon and use my body weight to press the pump.

"Hurry up," Bald hisses. "Or let me pump and you hold this thing."

"No. I'm too short to stand in the water. I'm almost done."

Slowly the boat unfolds and takes shape. When the third section is pumped Bald lets go of the motor. "Okay, now let's get my bag," he says.

"Get in. We'll take the boat to the gate, then we get your stuff."

The motor starts right up on my second pull of the starter cord. I cruise to the point above the tidal gate and quickly dart below to get his package. He won't steal my boat, not while I have his drugs.

Bald and I share only one goal: to get away from this burned-out mill as soon as possible.

24

HE'S GONE

MINDY

MOM AND I WAIT IN THE VISITOR CHECK-IN LINE AT THE HOSPITAL. There's so much we should be saying to each other, but we've never been able to talk through our masks. After that, I follow her up a long green hall. I skip along next to her until we get to intensive care. It seems busy for this time of the morning. The waiting room is packed. Efficiently, doctors and nurses flit quickly in and out of clearly marked areas. I do not see a uniformed police officer anywhere.

"This is ridiculous," Mom says. She steps in front of a nurse holding a clipboard.

"Can you help me? I think my husband is in here. Last name is MacKay. Could you check?"

Mom watches her scan a list on her clipboard.

"Oh. Here he is: Doctor MacKay. He's not in ICU anymore," the nurse says. "Follow me, please."

Mom and I exchange thumbs up. We follow the nurse and pass caregivers and people who hurt as much as I do inside. If I find out Dad is dying, this anxious fog in my head will lead me to a cliff over which to hurl myself. The patients have overflowed the wards and beds are lined up along the hallway. All the medical equipment hooked up to the beds is on wheels. Everything can move, but nothing does. Then I see him.

"Dad!" I shriek, and run to his bedside. I adjust the oxygen clip and tubing pulling on his nose. He groans. His eyelids flutter.

"Really? This is where you put Doctor MacKay?" Mom declares, staring down the weary nurse.

"We're overcrowded, as you can see," the nurse says. "We temporarily move patients like your husband into hallways until a bed frees up in a ward that can manage his condition—"

"What condition?" Mom demands. She sidles up to the bed without giving the nurse time to answer. "Oh, Lucas, honey, how are you?"

The nurse looks around and twirls her fingers in the air, hoping to get noticed by a doctor. "We'll see if Doctor Patel can take a look at his chart," she says.

An impossibly young doctor approaches. Her shiny black hair falls over her white coat bearing the name tag that says *Dr. Swati Patel.* However, as she reads the chart at the end of the bed, it appears to me that she knows what she's doing in spite of her perfect lipstick—I have to practice that—and the chaos in the hallway.

She looks up. "How are you folks?"

"From the look on your face, Doctor, I'm worried," Mom says.

A small smile. "Well, this is concerning. I see he's a doctor, so we're assuming his opiate withdrawal is deliberate. I see he's already delusional, though he's no longer on suicide watch. However, we are monitoring his withdrawal carefully."

Why am I not surprised by that word, delusional? I saw that manic look last night when he was high, but he said this dope sickness could be worse. Is delusional pain what he meant? Is this really my fault? After all, I prevented him from taking that pill because I stole it. Still, I have made my father—who I love dearly —suffer. And it could get worse. "Doctor, will he come back? Can he be normal after this?" I ask.

"Yes, what *is* his prognosis, Doctor?" Mom asks, stoking Dad's hand.

"Right now, hard to say. We expect him to purge the opiates in a few days, but stabilization could take as long as a week. He needs to washout—it's what we want for addicts. But we also need to get him out of here and into detox therapy as soon as possible. This is obviously not a safe environment."

"You think? In the hallway?" Mom blurts.

"See if you can check him into a longer-term inpatient rehab program, or an intensive outpatient program," Doctor Patel says. "If they can take him. And if not, have him recover at home. Some agencies have 'at home' detox and opioid treatment."

"I don't know if we can deal with this at home," Mom says, looking at dad like he's dog barf. "Can't we find him a ward?"

"There's just no space, as I said." She throws out her hands. "This speaks for itself. We're giving every patient the attention they need. Unfortunately, our focus has to be on new variant cases."

"Great," Mom says with a classic eyeroll.

"Mom! That could be us. Look around—there're doing the best they can. Thank you, Dr. Patel."

The doctor shoots me a little smile. "Look, we're not going to throw him out, okay?" she says. "We need the beds, but to be honest, his prognosis is uncertain. These kinds of withdrawal need to be gradual—and his has *not* been."

"There must be a faster way for him to detox, surely doctor." Mom says.

"Time, Mrs. MacKay, that's what he needs. And rest. There might have been other options, but it's almost too late for those. It looks like he self-medicates, and his chart makes no mention of therapy with medically assisted treatment—what we call MAT, which includes Narcan, Suboxone, Subutex, Vivitrol, Methadone, etcetera."

I remember Dad saying, "I am my doctor", so was the pill I stole from him one of those? Did he have illegal prescriptions for the drugs in his car?

"Also, the hospital is detecting sporadic contamination," Dr. Patel says. "So, the detox drugs are being held back and only used as a last resort, pending an investigation."

Mom shakes her head. "Really? How many more ways are there to prevent saving lives? How can you have bad drugs at a hospital? "

"That's a good question," Dr. Patel says. "The FDA has notified us to hold them until they have identified the source. So, we use other less effective antidotes, which I suspect is why your husband is in such bad shape. The thing is, antidotes can be abused to sustain addiction. I wonder, is that the case with your husband?" Doctor Patel asks.

"Of course not," Mom snaps. "He's a doctor."

She nods. But if the doctor asked me, I would ask, *Is that what's going on with Dad?* Or, would I cover for him like Mom does?

A nurse silently steps in front of Mom to adjust Dad's IV. "We've made him as comfortable as he can be," the nurse says, meeting Mom's frowning glare.

"Thank you, Nurse," Doctor Patel says. "And, please check on the nurse rotation so he's not missed because he's out here."

"Oh, good God," Mom says, "Please, get him into a ward and

out of this hallway! Mindy, stay here with Dad, I'm going to see what I can find out."

She's ten feet away before either Doctor Patel or the nurse or I can object to her leaving me here.

This consult with the doctor seems to have come to an end. Though it's still early the nurses and doctors are slouching from patient to patient—and Doctor Patel is no exception. They're worn out from the never-ending pandemic. And now this opioid crisis has buried them.

Meanwhile, Dad is still out. I take a moment to watch the slow rise and fall of his chest.

Well, I can help him.

If I was in his situation, I'd be anxious to know that my family was with me. I would not want to be forgotten. But I am not Dad. He's not going to call Mom. So, I'm going to call his sister Beth for him. I take his phone out of the clear plastic bag of personal stuff hanging off the foot of the bed next to his charts and bend down close to his face. He's out, but his breathing is regular. I get his phone to recognize his face after gently removing the nose-clip.

On his phone Beth is starred in Favorites. To make sure, I touch the icon photo to look for other information about her. Under *Work* I see an LA map. California. But what surprises me is that she looks younger than I imagined. The photo shows her with short-cropped blond hair—not what I'd expected.

Then I return the clip in Dad's nose. I can't do that again, and I can't turn off face recognition without his password. I don't have much time before his phone goes to the lock screen so I text Beth's details to my own phone. Then call on his phone.

A woman's voice: "Lucas. I was hoping you'd call."

"Aunt Beth, it's me, Mindy, your brother's daughter."

"Oh." Does she even know who I am? The connection hisses for a moment. "Is he okay?"

"No. He's overdosed. I wanted to let you know."

"Overdosed? Is he alive?" she asks in a high, scratchy voice.

"Yes, he's here at the hospital. I thought he'd want you to know."

Dad's eyes open. "Is that Beth? Let me talk to her."

So, he *has* been listening, which makes me wonder how out of it he really is. He could have thanked me for coming to see him or for calling Beth. Just a *thanks, Mindy,* would be enough. Instead, he takes, and takes. Like a child. But I need to be fair. How can he possibly love me when he's so sick?

I hold Dad's phone to his ear. I know he's still listening because his head is nodding ever so slightly and his eyeballs are moving under his lids. Suddenly, like he's just woken up, he croaks out, "Beth, I'm going now—" and drifts off again.

I stare at his face and wonder if he got anything Beth said, but he appears to be out of it. I disconnect the phone because I need to use the bathroom.

WHILE I'M WASHING MY HANDS, I REMEMBER I STILL HAVE DAD'S phone in my pocket. I need to call Beth back on my own phone.

She picks up. "Hello?"

"Sorry. I needed to go," I say. "This is my phone."

"You left him? Where are you?"

"Washing my hands in the bathroom."

"You disconnected me." She's outraged.

"Sorry. I didn't realize you wanted to hear me pee."

"Well no. But I did want to tell you, your dad is doing the right

129

thing. He wants to rid the world of evil and will do what it takes, even if he must manipulate the system. He's a good man. It might not seem like it, but he's protecting you. Does he tell you about his projects? The deep-sea fish farm and the medical research they're doing there?"

"No. But I love that he's working on that. It's about sustainable fish protein for the future, right? I've read about it." But no, he doesn't tell me anything anymore.

"Yeah. The research they're doing helps people like me," Beth says, then pauses. "You know I've had my ups and downs with drugs, right? So Lucas' vision is a god-send to people with addiction problems, which I used to have. Anyway, I'm coming to visit him."

"I hope you're not too late," I say.

"What do you mean?"

"Coming from California. He's hardly even conscious. Last night he was helping people who overdosed."

"Yes, I know. But I'm driving from Manhattan. I'll be there in two hours max. Tell your mom I'm coming. See you soon, okay?"

"Okay, Aunt Beth."

I dry my hands and fling the used paper towel away as questions crowd my head: Why have I never heard about these projects? Why was he calling Beth while he was on house calls? How exactly is he manipulating the system?

WHEN I RETURN TO THE HALLWAY, HIS BED IS GONE. I DO NOT see him.

Perhaps they moved him. I poke my head into the closest ward.

Several patients are hooked up to equipment. The ventilators are wheezing in and out.

"You can't be in here," a nurse says and ushers me back into the hallway. "What's your last name?"

"MacKay. My mother went to find out if they had a bed for my dad, Doctor MacKay."

"Stay here. We'll find your mother. Then we'll find your dad." The nurse gets on her phone. I hear a garbled announcement over the PA system. My mind can't let it go—what is Dad's vision? Whatever it is, it can wait. Right now, he needs my help. "I need to talk to Doctor Patel," I say to the nurse.

She frowns at me. "*She's* his doctor? She's a pediatrician—"

"Yes. I have information she needs."

"Like what? Are *you* okay? I'll call. Wait here," she says.

Dad is missing.

I speed dial Mom, but it goes to message.

I'm relieved to see Doctor Patel approaching. She seems dead serious. "Melinda, we're looking for your father. The whole hospital is. He's not answering his calls."

"I have his phone, but I can't login."

She looks at me as if to scold me, but then says, "Come with me to talk to the supervisor—she's talking to your mother."

Going up the elevator, I decide now is the time. I unfold the broken pill out of the tissue. "Doctor, this pill might be from that source everyone is looking for."

"I know you want to help, but why do you have this?" the doctor says, bending to take a closer look. She looks at it and grimaces. "The capsule is broken. What can they do with that?"

"They can match the chemical forensics, can't they? Maybe you could tell the detective for me?"

"I could, but did you steal this from your dad?"

"I did. Because all he wants to do is sleep after he takes them, though now that I know more, I think he was actually overdosing."

"Oh, you poor girl. He's alive. We'll find him." She takes the pill in the tissue. "I'll give this to the sheriff who was looking for your dad."

The elevator dings and opens. I'm going to trust Dr. Patel to keep this between us. She did not seem to like Mom much.

When we enter the office, Mom springs out of her chair.

"Mindy! Where were you?"

"Where were *you?*" I counter. "You just abandoned me. And you never answer your phone. Where's dad?"

"You were in the care of your father. You weren't abandoned."

"Thanks a lot, Mom. You leave me with Dad. All he does is lie there. He can't take care of himself—never mind me. And now he's gone. Here, take his phone. I didn't want to leave it at the end of his bed."

Mom takes it, shakes her head and looks at the ceiling.

The supervisor clears her throat. "So, neither of you know where Doctor MacKay is?"

Mom's face is a mask of politeness. Her little grimace tells me she really doesn't know, but she says, "Home?"

I take a deep breath. I can't tell Mom that I suspect Aunt Beth knows something about Dad's disappearance. Life is complicated enough without bringing Beth up, but I know I must tell her Beth's about to show up, because if I don't, she'll diss me to Mom.

My phone rings again. It's not Beth calling back—it's Pablo!

"I'm on Peter's boat," he tells me. "Tell the detective—"

In the background I hear a nasty voice, "Give me that phone."

Then his phone dies. I call back but it does not connect.

"Who was that?" Mom asks.

With Dad gone, this is not a good time to mention Pablo. "Marketing call," I say.

He's in trouble. I'll text Rennecker or Pablo's mom when I can —they need to know he's okay, though it didn't sound like he was.

But first, we should check on Dad. He could be in bed at home.

25

124 MILES AN HOUR

PABLO

WITH BALD UP FRONT IN THE RIB I'M BOATING UP THE INLET
toward the marina. Now is the first chance I have to call Mindy.
"I'm on Peter's boat. Tell the detective—"

"Give me that." Bald lunges at me and grabs my phone. He
tosses it into the water. I twist the throttle all the way and jerk the
tiller handle hard left. The inflatable lurches forward at an angle so
I can see if there's any chance of retrieving my phone. But the
water is black and flowing and it's useless. Bald has been flung
into the opposite edge of the boat but manages to grip the handle
on the side. He recovers quickly, jumps me, and wrestles the tiller
from my grasp.

He's stronger than he looks. I draw in a breath and hold it,
briefly figuring my chances if I jump and swim back to shore.
Then I remember Peter's phone is in the hatch.

"You're a loser," I tell him.

"Nice try," he huffs. Then he revs the motor in a tight U-turn
and heads out of the inlet. "Get up front, where I can see you."

He keeps his eyes on me as he holds his phone to his ear.
"We're good to go . . . Sound . . . midpoint from the mill."

I'm so done with him. It's time to go our separate ways. If I'm going to survive this I need to out-smart him.

~

ONCE WE CLEAR THE INLET, HE HITS THE SWELLS AT FULL throttle. It takes all my strength to hold on. The boat skims over the swells, taking each hill of water with the bow digging in and then rising over the crest. Each swell causes a plume of spray that smacks my face and stings my eyes. We hydroplane down and into the next trough. And so it goes. Soon, when we are far out in the sound, Bald cuts the engine.

If this is where he throws me overboard, I'll jump him and take my chances.

But Bald smiles and says, "Now we wait. Is there an anchor?"

"The anchor won't work," I say. "It's too deep."

"Get it out. Right now."

This works for me. Peter's phone is in the hatch with the anchor. Knowing Bald is watching me, I reach in for the anchor chain, play it out, and let it fall at his feet. With each length I pull out I move the Ziploc bag closer while memorizing the password. Finally, with the bag open, I slip the phone into my pocket and pull out the anchor.

"Good," Bald says. "Now throw it over. It'll slow our drift. Hurry. They're coming."

Within seconds a long, thin launch throttles back and glides to within a few feet of the RIB. A line is thrown out to Bald. He holds up the bag of drugs that I retrieved.

"Is that everything?" a man shouts over the guttural grumble of three motors boiling the water at the back of the boat.

"Yes," says Bald.

"And the boy?"

I do a second take. It's Sockeye. My stomach churns. I can't breathe. I vomit over the side.

"He helped me. I didn't want to leave a witness," Bald says, almost apologetically.

"Get them in here," Sockeye commands a crew hand.

They pull Bald and me into the launch.

"So, what now?" Bald asks Sockeye.

"You mean now that you've messed up the mission?" Sockeye asks. "You and the boy are going to explain yourselves to management."

"What about my boat?" I demand.

"He speaks," Sockeye says. "Here, let me show you." From his pocket he produces a red Swiss Army knife. It must be mine. He opens out the blade.

"Pull it in," he says to the crew hand.

Sockeye plunges the blade in and slashes it. Pressured air bursts out in a dying gasp. The crew hand throws the rope back in my sinking boat.

"Wave goodbye to it, kid," he says and pulls away.

He attaches his seat belt in the skipper's seat and the boat roars off. Within seconds my RIB is gone from sight, but not sunk, because, as Peter showed Dad and me, all three sections would need to be punctured to sink it. They could still find it with Bald's fingerprints on the motor cover. Oddly, I'm grateful to Bald that he did not explain to the arrogant Sockeye how I'd saved his life. I remember that Bald's wife and kids are being held by whoever 'management' is; he too is a victim of something more horrible even than Sockeye.

My objectives and Bald's are once again aligned, but I'm not going to be fooled twice—I need him to reveal our destination. However, the deafening roar makes talk impossible.

The crew hand throws oilskin rain jackets at me and Bald. "Strap yourselves in. They want you both alive."

They could have fooled me the way Sockeye treated Bald earlier—tying him up and throwing him under the mill. But maybe they just wanted to scare him. I put on the huge jacket, slip my hands inside the roomy sleeves, and scrunch down. This allows me to enter the password into Peter's phone. Then I press *record* in the *voice memos* app and hope the iPhone mic picks up any conversation. It's a long shot against the deafening motors.

"Where're we going?" I shout.

In a big voice the crew hand says, "They're going to feed you to the sharks outside the fish farm." He points. "Half-way to Bermuda—three hundred and seventy-three miles from here. We'll be there in three hours. Pretty good, huh? That's over one hundred and twenty-four miles per hour, so stay buckled up."

The motors roar. The g-force pushes me back into the seat. The wind rips at my jacket. Under my feet I feel the vessel take flight over the swells.

I do not have much time before I lose the cell connection on Peter's phone. Feigning terror I tuck my head inside the jacket and text Mindy, *help me.* I send the text with the VOICE MEMOS recording attached.

I have no idea if the recording will get through to Mindy. And if it does, and is usable, will she listen to it right away? And if she does, how can she bring it to the police as evidence that my dad was with Peter, when Dad's fishing gear was gone? Given these uncertainties, I'd rather conserve the phone battery. Tracking us with one bar showing is a long shot, so I power down the phone. My time is running out.

~

THERE IS NO LAND. THE DEEP, BROAD OCEAN SURROUNDS THE FOUR
of us. The big sky could not care less about me. The roar of the
boat's motors and the fumes from the gas tanks have dulled my
senses and prevented me from asking questions of the two men in
this boat. They both hate me. I must survive this race to my death,
and at one hundred and twenty-four miles an hour it will soon be
over. Counting down the miles does not help. What's the point? I
should have made a bigger scene at the mill. I should have jumped.

At last, the half-dome shape of the fish farm rises out of the
ocean haze, and then, on the horizon a distant shape of a large ship
emerges.

Mindy will be waking. She'll wonder if her dad is alive. If I am
alive. Mom will be researching everything she can think of on her
laptop. Peter will be walking Candy to the top of the rise. Detective
Rennecker will not know that I tried to call, then texted the
recording to Mindy. And not one of the them will know I am about
to become food at a fish farm in the middle of nowhere.

What prompts me to peek out of the oilskin jacket again is that
the momentum slows and lurches me forward as the boat drops to
cruising speed. As we approach the fish dome I'm gasping for air,
though there's more fresh air here than I've ever known. I crunch
into a tight ball with my arms clinging to my chest and bury my
head in the jacket.

The boat doesn't stop at the dome. The ship is growing in size
as we approach. At first it seems as high as our school, then closer,
double that, then double that again. Soon the vessel towers over us
as we pull alongside a gaping sea-level cavern opening up in the
side of the ship.

A gaggle of squawking marine radios hail men the height of

Pitbull dogs into the immense doorway. I prepare to give up the jacket and sneak Peter's phone into my sock, sliding it down next to my heel in my shoe. Lines are thrown and the launch is secured.

"C'mon," the crew hand says. He lifts me and passes me to a jovial brute on the ship who grabs my arm with one hand and lands me next to my frenemy. Bald.

26

THE RECORDING

MINDY

MOM PULLS INTO OUR EMPTY GARAGE.

"He's not here," I say. Obviously.

"His *car* is not here. Go check the house. Quick," Mom says. "I'll make some calls. We might have to drive to the police station. Maybe the hospital released him to the police for questioning."

I rush upstairs, but the hope has long been drained out of me. Their bedroom is quiet in its deathly perfection. I sit on their bed. Dad—my father, Doctor Lucas MacKay, is missing, which I don't think is true. He's not the type. But we never know with him these days.

I find Mom in the kitchen drinking water from a long glass.

"Why would he just leave the hospital, Min?" she asks.

"Do you think he did? You heard what that doctor said—his prognosis is uncertain. I think he's still there, somewhere. I just hope he's getting the right treatment because he's desperate for more pills."

"You make him sound like a teenage junkie, and that's just not your dad."

I swivel to face her squarely.

"What?" she asks.

"You don't get it. Why do you think he comes home in the afternoon, then goes back to work after dinner?"

"Why do you think you're not alone in the afternoons? I can't be with you because of my obligations to the hospital."

Of course; how could I forget? "Is that what he tells you?"

"Well, he also rests because of that damned accident. And the drugs knock him out."

"Mom, what if he has no pain?"

"That would be great if those drugs did their job."

"They have *no job to do*. He seems fine without his arm in that sling. I don't think he's in pain," I spell it out for her. "I think he likes those painkillers."

I'm surprised Mom does not come back at me with a cutting remark. She stares out of the kitchen window and slowly sips from her glass. Eventually she faces me, her demeanor calm.

"That's not fair, Mindy. He's a doctor. He knows better."

I give up. She can't face the truth. "Did you check his medicine cabinet?"

"Of course," she snaps.

I close PopJam and the bad news that awaits the people of this town.

"How about his pants?"

"Cut it out. It's not funny," she says, smacking the glass down on the counter.

"I agree. I wasn't joking."

The *bing* of an incoming text jolts me to my feet. Has Beth arrived?

Actually, it's from Pablo—with a voice memo attached. All the text says is *Help me*. I open the file. I put the phone on speaker and hit *Play*. I hear hissing and maybe a voice, but I'm not sure.

Mom waives my phone away for me to turn off the noise.

"I'm calling the detective," I say.

"I think you need some sleep," Mom says.

"Yeah. That would be nice."

Rennecker picks up. "Mindy. I heard from the hospital. Your dad's missing."

"I know. Mom's here with me. I also have a text from Pablo. You need to look at it."

"What's it say?"

"It says *help*. But there's a voice memo attached. All I hear is hiss on the recording."

"You're at home?" the detective asks.

"Yes."

"Okay, put me on *speaker*."

"Here's the thing, Mom," I say. "We have to act. Right now. Pablo's Mom needs to hear what's on his message." Then I switch on *speaker*. "Go ahead," I say to Rennecker.

"Mrs. MacKay, I want you to bring Melinda over to Peter King's house."

Exactly.

"Why would I do that?" Mom asks.

I'm tired of this too, Mom, I want to tell her. But I feel annoyed. Pablo has done something wonderful. Before I switch to *speaker* I need to urge her to keep on top of this, to not dismiss what he's done.

"Pablo's mother is here," Rennecker says. "She working with the FBI investigative team. She should hear her son's message first —if we can clean it enough to hear his voice."

"What about my husband?" Mom asks. "Any progress on *his* case?"

"We have no leads at this time," the detective says. "But when you and your daughter are here, let's drill down a little deeper with Mindy—with your permission, of course. Can you leave now?"

"Yeah, yeah," Mom says as she throws a pair of jeans onto the bed. "Sergeant major."

"Thank you," Rennecker says.

The connection dies.

~

WHEN MOM KNOCKS ON PETER'S FRONT DOOR THERE'S NO response.

"She did say Peter's place, right Mindy?" Mom asks.

"Look at all these cars. They must be around the back," I say.

A quick peek through the living room window tells me why they're not coming to the door. The floor is covered with boxes— many more than before. "There's no access even if they heard the door," I say to Mom.

In the backyard, I'm surprised to see a small crowd of people eating sandwiches and sipping chilled lemonades. Fred, Pablo's dad, is splayed out on the grass. Candy sniffs the hat over Fred's face, but he's asleep it would appear. I, on the other hand, am guiltily lifted by the brittle sunlight and cool fall air blowing over the sunflower field. Sanchia waves at me as she walks over to give me a high five.

"We going to get our boy back?" she asks me.

"Definitely," I say as confidently as I can. "And my dad."

Peter winks hello and nods at Mom, who frowns at him, though she does bump elbows with Sanchia.

"Penny. Call me Penny," Mom says. "If we're going to get your son and my husband back, we might as well be on a first-name basis."

"When we get them back," Sanchia corrects.

"That's right," Mom says.

Mom has met her match. These two women are saying *we*; working together they could be scary good.

The detective approaches me holding her hand out. "Let me have it." She takes my phone. She and Sanchia are right—there's no time to be nice. "Excellent," the detective says. "Let's go in."

We follow the detective through the house that is now, I realize, crammed with the belongings of the Cruz family. They have not been sitting around moping over Pablo. For the last twelve hours they've been moving into Peter's house, and I'm dying to know why. No wonder Fred is passed out on the lawn.

"I'm guessing, Peter, you don't want to move out?" I say.

"No, you got it," he says. "All things being equal . . . and they never are . . . but, this is right for me. I'll fill you in later."

It's weird how I know he's made the right decision. These are lovely people who'll look after him. And he'll look after them.

At the kitchen table a mask-wearing nerdy dude gets up from his laptop and takes my phone from Rennecker.

"This is our FBI electronics tech," she says. "He'll work his magic."

"Please login and open the audio file," he tells me.

He sets up on the counter, connects my phone, and then clamps headphones over his ears. Rennecker hovers. Mom sighs and sits.

"Why?" the detective asks Mom. "Why does a patient disappear? We know this happens with suspects, even when they are under surveillance. But him running out?" She sneers and shakes her head. "Did they check the morgue?"

"What? Good God no," says Mom. "The supervisor would have known, surely."

I've been watching the dude with an interesting screen up that

144

shows the graphical representation of the recording. I stroll over for a closer look.

"Hey," he says. "This spectral frequency editor shows the visual of the hiss . . . see the yellow banding? I can adjust the decay rate, like this." He takes off his headphones and previews the specific hissing noise he has cut out. "I'm going to save this extract, because to me, it sounds like several outboard motors, but we'll see. Detective, want to listen to this?"

She and Mom come over to look at the screen, though all we have to do is listen to the low-sound-quality voices on the recording.

"Where're we going?" That shout was Pablo.

Then, from a big voice, "Afterwards, they'll feed you to the sharks outside the fish farm."

Then something unclear, a pause, then, "Halfway to Bermuda . . ."

Something else I can't make out, then, "there in three hours…"
Then, "That's over one hundred and twenty-four miles per hour, so stay buckled up." The rest is hiss.

The detective notices Mom nodding her head slowly. "What are you thinking, Mrs. MacKay?"

"Deep-sea fish farming—my husband's project."

"Three hours," the tech says. "Has to be a rumrunner."

I guess I'm frowning at him.

"It's nothing new. Speedboats have been smuggling bootleg since Prohibition. Time stamp is 9:34." He looks at his watch. "They'll be arriving soon."

Rennecker leans over the tech and quietly says, "Find fish farms between here and Bermuda."

27

THE FISH FACTORY

PABLO

I'M SHOVED ALONG BY SOCKEYE, BALD, AND THE GANG FROM THE bottom of the ship up galleys and through thick metal doors till we come into a large, cold white space vibrating with industry and the smell of fish. The hum and clank of conveyer belts and packaging machines echo off the twenty-foot-high ceiling of pipes, bright lighting, and refrigeration vents. Men in bright yellow waterproofs handle the slithering silver three-foot fish as they process each down to shrink-wrapped slices on polystyrene platters, which they throw into boxes of dry ice.

We climb more stairs and come into a quiet and orderly observation deck. Bald shakes the hand of the bearded and rotund operational manager. I, of course, am ignored. Through the slanted window I look down on the processing plant we just came from.

"Come away from the glass, please," the manager says, then lowers his voice and asks Sockeye, "What are they going to do with him?"

Sockeye points at Bald. I turn my back on them as if I can't hear.

"He'll be part of the program—in the underage testing control group," Bald mutters.

The ops manager shakes his head and presses his lips together. "Okay, Jordan, after my China shipment is off-loaded, we load the boxed fish. Nineteen hundred hours, back here, okay? Get some rest," he says, dismissing Sockeye.

His name is Jordan? I make a mental note to find out where he's bunking. I want my knife back.

The manager hands something to Bald. "The boy is your responsibility, so you two will share the guest quarters," he says, stabbing Bald's chest with a commanding finger.

I draw in a deep breath and rub my eyes. How can I be fish food if Bald needs me for his program? Could it be worse than death?

LATER, BALD PRODS ME AWAKE IN THE BUNK HE'S ASSIGNED ME. "Hey . . . hey, kid, wake up. You hungry?"

I jolt upright. A cold fog clears my head as I remember I'm on a floating fish factory ship. I rub my hand over my face to wipe away beads of sweat around my mouth. Yes, I'm hungry. This ship must have all the services to support the men who work here—I haven't seen any women. And this man, this doctor of pharmacology who I have been calling Bald—because he is— seems to be looking out for me. He's prodded me awake and is treating me like I'm a lab rat for his experiments. He doesn't want to lose me.

But he will. Bald wants his family back.

"Did you find your wife and daughter?" I ask.

"You don't know about them, okay? Go take a shower, then get

147

lunch in the mess. Come to the observation deck when you're done."

My mouth is dry, and if Bald hadn't woken me my growling stomach would have. The quarters, as the manager called them, are quite comfortable—not like Mindy's bathroom, and this shower and everything is definitely not for the laborers down there on the factory floor. Doctor Bald carries some weight on this ship, which makes me dress quickly to get away from him. Peter's phone is still there—tucked into my shoe under my sock, hiding in plain sight.

Bald gives me directions to the mess and explains that it's not a mess, it's a kitchen and dining hall. "If you get lost, ask someone. Everyone knows where it is."

When I enter it's quite tidy. The mess is deserted but for a couple of stragglers who ignore me and mumble into their soup. The cook, scraping down the short-stack plate, greets me in Spanish—much to my relief.

"Why are they letting you wander around unsupervised?" he asks me, speaking English.

"Where am I going to go?" I say.

"Why? You want to run away?"

Actually, yes—but I don't say that. I do say, "I'm hungry."

"Want a burrito?"

My mouth waters. "Love one," I say. "But not fish. Can you do that?" I've lost my appetite for fish—since they might soon be feeding on me.

The cook smirks. "You're in luck, my friend. I have pulled pork."

"Oh yes, thanks. And after, can you show me how to get outside?"

He nods as he works on my meal. I sit on a steel chair at a long steel table next to his work station. Unless I'm going crazy, this cook is friendly—in a good way. But can I trust him?

"Here you go," he says and places a large plate on the pickup counter. "I made them chimichanga style for you."

The three lightly fried pork burritos sprinkled with lime and served with a side of fiery salsa, beans, and rice drives me almost insane it is so delicious.

"Good?" he asks.

"Man, this is so good. Thank you so much, sir," I say. "This is excellent."

"Juan. Call me Juan. You?" he asks, pointing at me.

"Pablo."

"Who are you with?"

"The doctor," I say.

I can't call him Bald and I don't know his name. But it doesn't matter.

Juan wrinkles his nose and tilts his head to one side. "Which one? The pharmacy guy?"

I nod.

He takes my plate. "This is not a cruise ship, Pablo. Be careful. But come. I'll show you a way outside." He leads me through the mess kitchen to a rear door with a keyless combination deadbolt pad, and says, "Nine-two-four-three, if you need to get in and I'm not here."

Why would he say that? First, he tells me to be careful, but he doesn't know Bald the way I do. Then he gives me a place to hide.

The door opens into a large storage room with shelves lined with canned and bottled food and cardboard boxes of root vegetables stacked in front of large walk-in refrigerator doors. There's a paperwork-strewn table serving as a desk with a computer monitor. Juan sits and taps the number keys on his keyboard. The screen displays his Gmail. With an Internet connection I can message home. And Mindy.

I want to tell Juan about the characters I've designed for the game, about my beautiful, smart mother and my brave father. And about Mindy, who needs my help. But I hesitate; it's too soon. I can't even risk asking him for a charge of Peter's phone. What if he turns me over to the operations manager?

I look around and say, "This ship is bigger than my school."

"I know, right? We feed everyone on this ship—breakfast, lunch and dinner, two shifts every day. And that includes the hospital for all the trawlers in the fishing fleet," he says pointing to the door. "I'll show you, come. 'Cause that's your way out. The nurses take the meals into the ward through this door. Remember, you never saw this hospital. They don't want the workers to know about it…at all, okay? There are so many accidents they can't hire enough workers. And that wacko pharmacy guy you came with puts them on painkillers that turn them into addicts . . . you'll see the nutjobs covered in sweat. There are COVID patients here too. Put this on," he says and hands me a plastic-wrapped mask. "Us Latinx guys got to stick together. I'm undocumented, just like you, I guess?"

"Yes. Thank you for helping me."

Why is the cook looking at me, assessing me? Is he wondering if he can rely on a Dreamer kid?

We enter a clean ward with rows of beds perfectly lined up, all hooked up to medical equipment. Juan hurries me through, warning me not to speak. But I do look. Every bed is occupied. In an operating theater at the other end a female nurse is checking the IV level of a patient. Juan tugs my sleeve. We exit through a heavy metal door onto an exterior gangway.

"Thanks," I say and drink in the energy of the oxygen-rich

breeze. I grab the railing—going over is a gut-wrenching drop into the churn and chop of the hungry waters far below. Not far off, a trawler half the height of the ship we're on is being buffeted by the swells. Its hull is open for the crane of the factory ship to peck out plastic-wrapped palettes of cargo that swing in the stiff breeze.

I've been gone too long and I need to get to the observation room. However, I can't resist taking a photo with Peter's phone, even though there is not much charge left. I zoom in and snap a photo of the name of the ship: *Jian Mei 5*.

"Chinese trawler," Juan shouts over the wind. "Brings medicines and drugs, food and supplies in exchange for packaged fish. And Pablo, stay out of their way, my friend. Don't let them see you taking photographs. Walk around and enter from the other side. Go. I'll see you soon. *Hasta la próxima vez.*"

That's right, Juan—till next time. Because maybe together we can find a way to get off this ship of secrets.

28

UPLOADING TO PARADISE

PABLO

CLINGING TO THE RAILING ON THE GANGWAY I MAKE MY WAY TO the bow and take in the immensity of this ship.

Above the buffeting wind I hear the faint thudding pulse of an approaching helicopter. Positioned as I am, crouched below the bridge on the narrow gangway, I watch the chopper wobble as a gust lifts its blades, but then it settles onto the helipad below. The rotors wind down and a sliding door opens. Passengers file out.

They're a gray, grim-faced bunch, lugging themselves and carry-ons, their hunched backs turned against the whip from the rotors. However, the short-cropped blond hair of a woman Mom's age stands out. She's assisting a man who staggers along, clutching her elbow. Because it's hard to see his face, I zoom in with Peter's camera and take a photo. When I preview it I'm looking at Mindy's dad, dressed exactly how I last saw him—chinos, a white open-neck shirt and a red sweater.

I must get these photos to the detective. They'll prove that Dad and I are not criminals, though they might prove that Mindy's dad is. That's not for me to decide.

I let myself in on the other side of the ship. Access from this side of the observation room is via a side door with a porthole window. To check before I open the door, I peer through.

A small group with their backs to me are gathered around the control console. Doctor MacKay in his red sweater stands next to Bald and a man wearing a Red Army Mao cap. I know this cap because Mom and I made it part of the design for our game character. He must be the captain of the trawler delivering the cargo. He is now adamantly pointing at an object on the console. It's a red a fishing tackle box. Yes, it's the same shape, size, and color as what I saw at the mill.

I duck away from the door, my hands shaking as I fumble the phone. Its charge is down to less than twenty percent—enough for one more photo of this group before I need to get these to Mom. Team Cruz will know what to do—our team motto is *Everyone for himself, provided Mom knows.* So now, as always, I will include her using our special method.

It's our own messaging system of making comments in our game development code—pointing out mistakes, broken links, and funky design from me. She doesn't like email and hates the trolls in social media. So, we stick to our secret comments in the code— it's our own thing—no lurkers chipping in, no judgmental eyes. No cat-voice videos.

This time however, my comment in the code will direct her to my uploaded photos.

I lift myself up to eye level and take the photo, then I back away.

Now I can't go into the observation room. Doctor MacKay will recognize me. I quickly scan the photos, then come back to the one with the nurse coming off the chopper, helping Doctor MacKay. The detective might have enough now.

I run back to the guest quarters and prepare to be sleeping

when Bald returns. I power down the phone and slip it into my shoe, like before. For a moment I rest my eyes and pretend to be asleep. Then I am.

～

I AM WOKEN LATER BY VOICES. BALD IS SAYING GOOD NIGHT TO someone but is having a hard time with it. He staggers to his bed but changes his mind and leans over my face. I try to control my breathing through my nose. His breath smells of liquor. I wait, then he grunts and moves away. I hear the heavy thud of his body landing on his bed. He groans once. I wait. Soon the snoring begins, deep, long, and endless. Perfect.

I slide out of the bunk and carry my shoes and phone out of the suite. The passageway has low red safety lighting, though I can remember the way to the mess. Still in my socks I pad through the dark dining area, past benches, kitchen counters and cooktops to the back and stop at the keyless deadbolt pad. I push in nine-two-four-three, and the lock whines open. I enter and make sure the door closes behind me and stand still in the blackness. The desk is lit by tiny pricks of jeweled computer lights.

My breath comes short and quick as I fumble for Peter's phone and power it on. The phone now shows ten percent charge. In front of me I touch Juan's keyboard and am prompted for a password. There's only one possibility to try that has a shot of working. It does. Nine-two-four-three worked; Juan is a nice guy, but he's got a lot to learn about security.

I text Mom: *Uploading to paradise*

I transfer the photos to Juan's computer, log in to our gaming cloud and upload them. Now it doesn't matter if the phone dies. Mom and Detective Rennecker are on the job.

29

OBFUSCATION

MINDY

SANCHIA PUSHES AWAY FROM WATCHING THE TECH'S SCREEN. SHE grabs her phone in her back pocket. "It's Pablo. Oh my God!"

Rennecker takes a step closer to look at Sanchia's phone.

"What's 'Uploading to paradise' mean?" the detective asks, confused.

With lightening fingers Sanchia texts back: *K*. "He's uploading to our development platform for our game, *Para Dize IV*. Smart guy." She places her laptop next to the tech's on the kitchen counter.

"Here they are," Sanchia says.

We crowd around her laptop and look at the photographs.

"Who is this woman?" Rennecker asks Mom.

Mom leans closer and frowns.

"It's Aunt Beth. And that's got to be Dad with her," I say, pointing.

Mom looks closer and slowly shakes her head. "Oh, Lucas, what have you done? How do know this is Aunt Beth?" she says to me.

"There's an ID photo of her in Dad's contacts," I say, pointing at her handbag. "On his phone. The same short blond hair."

Mom digs in her bag.

"You can't login, Mom, unless you have his password—or his face, which was how I opened his phone. So, he and Beth are working together. Why are all the tackle boxes the same?"

"We've seen these red tackle boxes on online," Sanchia says. "Fred almost bought one for under ten bucks. They sell out. Often."

"It's an obfuscation tactic," Rennecker says. "Fishermen refueling next to the mill don't attract any attention carrying those things because they all have them."

I lean forward and whisper to Mom, "What does ob-va-skating mean?"

"To make something confusing—obfuscation—even if it seems obvious. You should also google hide-in-plain-sight."

It sounds like what Dad does all the time.

The tech looks up from his screen. "Check this out," he says to Rennecker.

She reads. "The Blue Seas Project. That mean anything to you, Mrs. MacKay?"

"That's his," Mom says.

" Mrs. MacKay, there's a connection to your husband—if the Blue Seas is where they're headed."

"It's about three-hundred miles northeast of Bermuda," the tech says.

"Figures," Rennecker says. "FYI, we're now looking at this as one case, which includes Pablo and your husband, Lucas, as a persons of interest."

"That's nice, Detective. Are we spinning wheels? Because my son is still missing."

This is not the Sanchia I thought I knew. This is a no-nonsense, do-as-I-say mother who's not going to let this case focus on Dad. I get it. But I need to focus on both of them. Pablo must be in terrible danger—much worse, I'm guessing than Dad, who has more clout than smarts. Maybe they're both caught up in this... whatever this is. The facts are leaning that way.

"Who says we're waiting?" the detective says. "I've been contacted by the FBI Special Agent in Charge of this case. He recommends Mindy be available to supply information to their profiler. And you'll be needed there as well, Mrs. Cruz."

"Okay. Does that mean we'll have to go back to that awful police station?" Mom asks.

"No. They want Mindy in Bermuda."

"Bermuda?" Mom, Sanchia, and I say at the same time.

"Yes." Rennecker is serious. "It's the closest airbase to where they think the fish factory is. A parent must attend the interviews. Same with you, Mrs. Cruz, for Pablo, when we find him. The FBI will make reservations. Go home, pack light. They'll contact you. And, ladies, this is not a vacay, got it?" She points at the photo of the Chinese trawler. "The *Jian Mei 5* is being tracked via satellite. The source of those drugs in the fishing tackle boxes must be identified in order for us to close the case."

"And what are Fred and I going to do?" Peter says.

"Bond," Sanchia says. "Get the sunflower stand fixed up. We're going to have a killer season."

THE SHIP OF FOOLS

PABLO

ON JUAN'S PC IN THE DARK I DELETE THE BROWSER HISTORY OF my usage and wipe down the keyboard. Before exiting the back of the kitchen, I listen for voices and silently slip through the door, making sure I hear the deadbolt slide.

I find hope in the secret world where Mom and I communicate, playing God with our game characters. And now our made-up mythology has become real for both of us. My short messages and links to the photographs are thin attempts to reach out to her, but are as strong as spider silk. Like the terns, each file flies across hundreds of miles of sea. Each urgently posted photo endures the gales whipping the white horses, the drenching squalls, the electric storms that threaten to erase them.

Please come to get me, was my last message to her before I shut everything down.

Though it's still not sunrise, I hear voices as I return to the guest quarters on the ship. There's a shout of protest—it's Bald, pleading. They're looking for me too because another voice says, "He's not here." When they come around the passage corner, Bald is being hauled off his feet by a hefty dude. I recognize Sockeye's crew hand.

"There. Get him," Sockeye orders.

They're coming my way. I rush back into the mess. By the time they get through the kitchen area, I've entered nine-two-four-three. But it's too late. A boot blocks the door from shutting. Without turning on the lights, I find the hospital door and slip through just as they find the lights. From a nearby bed, off an overbed table I steal a metal bowl that will clang when the door opens.

Something else catches my eye, something I remember that helped me and Dad through many winters: baby oil. I place the bowl six inches in front of the door.

Where do I hide? There, next to the operating theater, a utility room with an electrical fuse box. It has janitorial supplies and a rolling canvas laundry cart filled with uniforms and blue scrubs. I could get in and cover myself to hide, but I hear the clang of the bowl.

Now is my chance. I grab some scrubs and run for the exit door, making sure I'm seen by my pursuers.

"Get him—"

Before Sockeye can finish cussing, I exit the exterior door and slam it shut, sucking in the briny air. The sun spills a sliver of gold over the vast tipping ocean. Working quickly, I squirt the oil over the three railings and empty the rest of the bottle over the deck in front of the door, making sure there are no dry spots. Then I wait at the side of the door.

The crew hand bursts through the door and his legs slip out from under him. He slides flailing toward the edge of the ship, his hands grasping then sliding off the railing. He falls away with outstretched arms, his bellowing voice lost to the wind.

Sockeye follows, unaware of what's just happened, but he's more cautious. He finishes his slide by managing to hold on to the lower rail. He's suspended above the churning sea below only by the strength of his hands.

"Hello," I say.

"You!" Sockeye shouts. "Pull me up."

"No. Give me my knife."

He huffs. His fingernails are going white, his face is reddening. "Pull me up, you little runt."

"The knife you stuck into my boat. It's mine. Give it to me." I tie the leg of a scrub around the railing, then I tie another leg to it, producing a rope of sorts—like in the comics. I dangle it over Sockeye's head. "Knife," I say.

He clenches his jaw and quickly grabs the knife out of his pocket while holding on with one hand. He throws it rattling across the oiled deck. "Now help me up. I'm dying here."

"I don't care, but I have one question before you go." I carefully step back to pick up my pocketknife.

"No, don't go. Don't go. Please," he shouts.

"Then why?" I demand.

"Why what? God damn it."

"Why do you want to kill the bald guy?"

"Because he screwed up a good plan; he tried to steal from the boss. He got greedy, okay? Now help me."

"One man runs everything? What about the captain?"

"No. The boss of the company, the boss of the ships, the boss of the syndicate is here. He came in on the chopper yesterday. And I promise you, I'll persuade him to save your life. Because they'll hunt you down."

So, "The Man," the person who everyone is so terrified of is actually Mindy's dad. I have photographs of him getting off that chopper, other photos at the observation deck wearing his red sweater. I've been in his house. I've seen his bedroom. I know his daughter. And everything I've seen about him tells me he's a pretender. Perhaps he is ruthless; I don't know. What I do know is that he has tons of money and he's powerful—and he's an addict. That's his big secret.

Sockeye is greedy and ambitious and wants to stay close to Doctor MacKay because he thinks his money will rub off on him. Maybe that's true. "Hey, you're in no position to make promises, okay? But I tell you what; if you're so close to him, why don't you tell him I have a source in a cartel. He'll never have to deal with China again."

I have his attention—in a new way, other than looking at me as his lifesaver. I have given him the opportunity to suck up to his boss.

I'm making a deal with the devil. I should let Sockeye fall to his death like his crew hand? I've already done something terrible, something I can never take back. That crew hand let me wear the big jacket on the boat and when he passed me over to the brute on the ship he made sure it was safe. Somewhere deep within him was a good man. He could have dropped me; I would have been another accident. No biggie. But he didn't.

Sockeye is the evil one—he's smuggled boatloads of poison into the East Coast. His pill mills have killed thousands of people. Stopping Sockeye with baby oil was no joke—it was self-defense. What would they have done with me? The death of Sockeye's crew hand will make no difference to him—if he lives. He'll get a replacement. I can't forgive Sockeye, though I should credit him for the plan taking shape in my head.

What's popped into my head is wrong in so many ways, not the least of which is that I'm using my Mexican heritage for the worst reason. The cartels murdered many of Mon's relatives. However, if I can get Doctor MacKay to leave the ship somehow, there'll be a chance to get Mindy's dad back, even if it means he might die from withdrawal, including withdrawal from this whole ugly business he's in.

Mindy will know that I tried for her. If this works, it'll mean I'll be free of this ship, and if I ever get to see Mindy again, I hope she'll be relieved to see me. But she'll be heartbroken that she lost her dad to his horrible scheme. Eventually, if I don't succeed, we'll drift apart, because when she sees me, she'll think I had a chance to pull him out of this mess, but I let her down. My heart hurts thinking about that. So, I'll try.

Sockeye's hands are slowly slipping around the pipe and he's panting like a dog. "Yes, I'll tell him," he shouts. "He won't believe me, but I'll tell him. Please, don't let me fall."

I place the leg of the scrub within his reach. I step back carefully so as to not slip, and I re-enter the hospital. As I close the door and lock him out, I hear him shout, "Where do I find you?"

I take off my shoes and head for the utility room next to the operating theater. A closet with freshly-laundered scrubs—men's and women's, plus blue surgical caps, offers me a range of options. There's also a pile of N95 face masks. I help myself to three. The women's size is a little big, but allows me to wear the blue pants (rolled up around my waist) and the top over my clothes. The surgical scrub cap fits too. From a distance, I'm now a nurse.

My stomach and a wall clock tell me it's breakfast time. I put on the cap and a face mask, grab a clipboard and stride out into the ward, like I own the place. I head for the kitchen storage room.

Juan is at his desk, ordering. I knock on the refrigerator door and he spins around. "Hello nurse . . . you? Had me fooled for a second."

"I know. Listen, Juan, you wanna get off this ship?"

He pushes his chair back and locks his hands behind his head. "I'm listening, but I can tell you there are only two ways: chopper or trawler. And trawler is not an option. You . . . " he shakes his head. "You won't survive."

"Actually, there's a third way. It's how I got here."

"The cigarette boat? What are you on, crack? That thing is Jordan's baby, man. He's at it twenty-four seven."

"So, he doesn't sleep? He doesn't go to the bathroom? He eats all his meals at the boat? We can jump on when he's on a break."

We both freeze when we hear a long ring of an alarm bell. Then another long ring, and another.

"That's man overboard," Juan says. "Three long blasts is MOB. Wait for the ship whistle . . . there, one, two, three. Definitely, man overboard" Juan stares at me. "They'll drop lifeboats. This means all hands on this ship. I wonder who fell."

Sockeye's survived and he's sounded the alarm to search for his crew hand. I'm eyeing the exits, expecting them to burst through. He's pulled himself up with my rope of dirty scrubs. So now, when he sees a medic in scrubs, he'll have the urge to murder me—or some nurse. But I can always take them off.

"It's Jordan's crew hand who fell," I say.

"What? How do you know that?"

"I helped him fall."

"I don't even want to know about it, okay?" he says, jumping up from his desk. "Man, you *are* trouble!"

"You got a better plan? You like it here, working for him?" I have Juan's attention; his wheels are spinning. "Think about it, no one's looking for me, not now. They'll wait until after the drill.

And if you're missing, your staff will say you're delivering food to essential workers. So, by the time they realize the boat is gone and not being skippered by Sockeye—I mean, Jordan—we'll be miles away, and nothing can catch that boat."

"Sockeye? That's good." He nods. "Well, now's the time— MOB is crazy. On this ship a drill like this means all hands, except essential workers, like me—people got to eat—and the engine room, senior officers." He looks at me in the scrubs. "And medics."

"So, now's our chance. You take a food delivery and we visit the man. If we can, we take Jordan's boat with the man on it. I want him to come with us. Make a run for Bermuda."

Juan puts his head back and laughs. "Please, stop kidding yourself. What do you think, the boss is going to jump on the boat because you want him to? Is this a joke? Why would he do that?"

"He's the father of my friend and he's gotten into drug running and can't get out. We have the opportunity to stop this. He wants to be back with his family, but there's huge money in this and he can't pull himself out. We can help him."

"No, we can't." Juan says.

"You can save lives if this works. All you have to do is show me the way to his cabin, deliver breakfast to him, do whatever, but get me access to him. I'll do the rest. If it doesn't work out, well, you were just delivering his breakfast."

Juan glares at me, but the possibilities are sinking in.

"We'll have to swing by the engine room. It's not far from where Jordan's boat is tied off. It's probably not being used because drills are lifeboats only."

~

WHEN WE ENTER HIS SUITE, DOCTOR MACKAY LOOKS AT ME, incredulous. "Who's the nurse, cook?" he says to Juan.

"We're just helping out where we can, sir, because of the ship MOB drill," Juan says, placing a wrapped breakfast burrito on his work desk.

"Well, kid? Have you treated anyone?" he says. He points at me and scowls. "Take off your mask."

My heart pounds in my chest. When I last him, he was wiping white powder from his nostrils like a hero at the top of his world, but right now his eyes are sunken. He clears his throat and scratches the back of his head.

"Doctor MacKay. My name is Pablo. I am Mindy's friend—"

"Mindy...yes, that's it. Thought I recognized you." He snaps his fingers and points at me. "I gave you a ride home and then you tricked me. You got me arrested, you little punk."

He takes a step toward me, but I dart over the bed to the other side.

He stops, shakes his head and smiles at me, almost like he's being friendly. "I remember now. Soccer player, right? Relax, kid —I'm not going to hurt you."

"Mindy got you arrested—that's how worried she was about you," I say. "She used me as her excuse to get you out of your bedroom and stop you taking any more pills."

"Okay, Pablo, cut the BS. Jordan already told me how you were about to send him swimming—good for you, by the way. I am impressed that you were able to trick two of my tough guys— but then you spared Jordan's life and sent him to me with a message. How the hell did you get here? Talk to me."

"I can't talk with the cook here."

He pulls a twenty from a roll and hands it to Juan.

"Thank you, Sir," Juan says as he walks out of the suite.

165

"So, Pablo. Tell me about the Mexican cartel. I'm interested."

"We can't discuss it here. The Chinese can't know about this."

"You're right."

"That's why we're going to borrow Jordan's boat," I say. "While he's doing the drill."

"You got this all worked out, don't you. Who are you working for?"

"We can discuss that later, but I will need a crew hand. Juan, the cook, could help right now, because he's not part of the drill. No one will know where he is because they'll think he's delivering food. Or will you help me with the tie-ups?"

"You don't need a crew," he says.

"Jordan has one."

He nods and presses his lips together.

"You mean had one—did you forget? Okay, bring the cook, and just so we're clear, if you try any stunts like you did with Jordan, I'll put a bullet through your head. After you." He waves me out the door, grabs a windbreaker and from under his pillow, a hand gun. "Let's blow this popsicle stand."

I have no clue how to crew the boat, but from what I remember, there's forward and backward and a throttle and a steering wheel. Juan will have to navigate.

As the alarms continue to sound, everyone scrambles past us to the upper decks while we make our way down, me in my medic scrubs, and Juan in his white cook's jacket, lugging a pizza delivery box over his shoulder. We hurry down the clanging stairs passing through deck after deck until we come to sea level.

In the cavernous space the drug-running boat is carefully

moored with clean blue and white fenders protecting the hull. There's no one around. We don't have a lot of time.

Mindy's dad is almost off this ship, which will be great for Mindy—and for me. But I'm not looking forward to telling him that we're taking the boat and him to Bermuda.

BERMUDA

MINDY

A SOFT KNOCKING ON THE HOTEL ROOM DOOR WAKES ME, BUT I can't get out of bed. I fall back to sleep, but again hear the two dull taps.

Mom had left the *DO NOT DISTURB* sign on the door, so whoever's out there isn't getting the message—and it's almost midnight.

I didn't sleep on the plane coming over from JFK. Mom was passed out from the time we took off until we landed on Bermuda two hours later. Our contact had us wait on standby in the JetBlue terminal all day and we only got onto a flight late in the afternoon. By the time we checked into the hotel, all the promised excitement of the brilliant bays, the beaches, and the spas had worn off. The hotel, compared to what I'd searched, was a dump. Google said it was an airport hotel, and reviewers said it was for one-nighters, but they said the bar scene was hot.

When we checked in, Mom promptly fought for an upgrade one floor up. She ordered room service for me and left me to sleep. If I needed help, she said I should call Clem—Special Agent in Charge of the FBI operation, Clement R. Horace, so his card says.

"Sanchia and I have our first assignment," she told me. "We'll be at the bar."

I can see Sanchia, steady and brilliant, hanging at a bar with Mom who's clicking her fingers at the barman.

I hear the two knocks again. Now I'm really awake and stomp to the door. "Who is it?"

"Me."

Pablo. I gasp, then pull him in and hug him close. His clothes are damp. "So good to see you."

"Oh man, you too! I thought I'd never see you again, Mindy. I've been waiting for your mother to leave."

"Why didn't you call or text? Your mom's here too, you know. How'd you find us?"

"Through your dad."

"My dad? What do you mean?"

"He called my mom. I heard him say, "Bermuda" and "FBI", so I called mayday on the marine radio. We were about a mile out from the shore. As the Coastguard approached your dad just sat there with his head in his hands. He wasn't even angry at me, and he had a gun. He could have shot me. But he thanked me and said I should go, and when I see you to tell you he loves you. Juan and I jumped and swam. We didn't want to be turned over to the authorities. When I finally had enough strength, I went around the back of another hotel and asked the kitchen staff where the FBI stay. A lady in housekeeping thought she knew. She didn't say why, but she was right."

"You snitched on my dad, Pablo. What kind of friend are you? How could you do that?"

"Your dad, the cook, and I had escaped the fish factory. If the Coastguard didn't pick him up, the Chinese drug-runners would have caught him."

"I can see you're kind of proud about what you did."

He hangs his head and nods. "I knew you'd hate me after I did that. But I realized, if he returned to you guys, his family, he'd carry on the way he had before. I'm sorry, Mindy; I had to do it." He looks up into my eyes. "I can't stand to watch how you go from day to day, worried sick about your dad. I hope we can still be friends."

I throw my hands up. "So now *you* decide what's best for us?"

"He's a wanted man anyway, and I didn't want to be caught. Think about it—he can now be treated for his withdrawal. I knew your mom wouldn't turn him in and you wouldn't disagree with her . . . you're too kind and you wouldn't want to punish her with the truth about your dad."

"And you know what the truth is," I snap at him.

"I've seen the evidence."

I shake my head, pulling my thumb in my other hand. "Yes, I saw the photos you uploaded. Well, let's go give them the good news that he's back—then the bad," I say. "I've been told I can't use my phone, but they're having a drink at the bar. I'm going to get ready."

In the bathroom I dress in black because that's what people do at night. And it suits what I'm thinking about the black water grabbing at Pablo as he swam to the shore. It must have been terrifying. How could he be so certain he was doing the right thing?

"Wow," Pablo says when I come out. "You got all dressed up for your mom?"

He's trying to be nice. "That's right, man. And you're in your wet Sunday school clothes from Saturday." I shake my head and snort. "Let's trash those. Go in there. Wash up. Here." I toss him a pair of my slim fit ripped denim stretch pants and mom's yellow loose fit tank top. She likes those because they make her look athletic. "Put these on. You can wear my denim jacket and flip flops."

While I wait, I try mom's lipstick, but now is not a good time to practice patience. I rub it off with my finger. I'm not Doctor Patel yet. I take a deep breath. The thing is, Pablo's random actions can be exasperatingly smart. He would not have risked his life to do this if he didn't value our friendship. I'll back off because he is a true friend.

Pablo saunters out sheepishly with his hands in his pockets to keep my jeans from falling down. I know he's sensitive about that —pants pulled down, falling down, whatever, because of what happened on the day I met him. I loved seeing him later that year at soccer practice, running circles around that boy who pulled his pants down. His revenge was his skill, not just with the ball, but with that boy. Pablo made him look like a fool.

"Wow. Mister Cool. Here's a belt." I roll the sleeves of my jacket off his wrists and decide that my jeans on him should drag over his flip-flops. Then I borrow a scoop of Mom's gel and comb his hair back with my fingers.

"Get off me," he says.

He looks like a sloppy hipster wannabe in an outfit I really can't stand, but I am a hundred percent sure he'll not be taken for the Pablo Cruz who dragged himself in here half an hour ago.

In the lobby an airline crew is checking in. Couples are coming in from somewhere else, going up the escalator. We follow them and come into the packed restaurant that opens onto a broad balcony overlooking the bay. The music pounds my eardrums. We bully through the crowd and catch Mom sitting at the bar, laughing with an older Asian gentleman. On the other side of him Sanchia leans across, talking to Mom.

"Mindy." Pablo leans in close to my ear. "That's him—he came off the trawler that brings in the drugs from China."

I recall the photo Pablo sent. Mom must be thinking the same thing: she can't screw up their assignment because he's key to finding out how Dad is involved.

"That's the captain in the photo?" I ask. "The one where Dad and the man in the Mao cap are looking at the tackle box?"

"I don't know if he's the captain, but I'm sure that's him," Pablo says.

The so-called captain has slung his jacket over the back of his bar stool, and with Mom and Sanchia on either side of him he feels no pain as he swishes an amber liquid in a thick glass. A quick peek inside his wallet will tell me who he is.

Mom and Sanchia look lovely, so in control, as if somehow each is the salve for the other's emptiness—the missing son, the missing husband. And for this I love them both. The laugh lines around Mom's mouth break as Sanchia slaps the counter with her palm and they shriek. The Asian man's hand squeezes Mom's forearm.

I've seen enough. "Pablo, go stand at the edge of the balcony and lean over. Look out at the bay. I'll let your mom know."

He nods and disappears through the crowd.

I hurry to them like I've just spotted them. "Good evening, ladies."

Mom swivels. "Mindy! You're up?"

Sanchia slides her stool out to kiss my cheek. "Hey, girlfriend. Look at you. Little touch of lipstick, there. Nice."

I push the suite key card under Mom's arm while my other

hand reaches into the inside pocket of the man's jacket. I extract the wallet. "I'm going to bed. Thought you'd need the key," I say.

"Yes. I do," she says.

I blow her a kiss as I pocket the wallet.

Sanchia hasn't missed a thing. "Mindy and I are going to the bathroom, Penny," she says.

We push through the crowd until I can no longer see the bar. I grab Sanchia's sleeve. "Pablo's here."

"What?"

"Come," I say. We break through the crowd and walk over to the balcony railing to gaze at the starry night over the bay.

"Look to your left," I say.

When their eyes meet, Pablo strolls over. He really is Mr. Cool, and I get that he doesn't want to attract too much attention, but they hug regardless.

"Sanchia, I have his wallet," I say interrupting them.

"I know," she says.

"You have the captain's wallet?" Pablo asks, surprised.

I nod. "I can't show you here."

"I need to go back," Sanchia says.

"You should go. If he's the captain, we'll take photos and I'll meet you back at the bar."

"Hurry. We don't know how many brandies he'll have before he leaves—or passes out."

BACK IN MOM'S SUITE, I SPLAY A GRID OF THE WALLET CONTENTS on the bed—so I can return them in the same order. Then I snap a photo.

"There," Pablo says, pointing at an International Certificate of

Competence. "Wouldn't he have that if he was the captain of the *Jian Mei 5?* That was the name of trawler at the factory ship. If this proves he's the Chinese trawler captain, they'll have what they need to shut down the fentanyl trade."

"We'll text this photo to Clem," I say.

"But what if that's not enough? We need to get into his room," Pablo says. "But we must be careful. These are dangerous people."

I nod slowly. This is a risky game we're playing. This is not soccer and it's not Pablo and Sanchia's computer game, though that game has been a clever tool in this case. But now we must finish the job. "I'm going to assume the captain would be right below us in the upgrade suite."

"Let's try it. What do we have to lose?" he says.

"Everything, but now's our chance."

We head down one flight of stairs. Pablo strolls into the passage then gives me an all-clear thumbs-up. I run and slide the card through. It clicks open.

The suite desk is strewn with paperwork—preapprovals, safety docs, waste declaration certificates and other reports. With my phone camera, I snap photos of the pages without touching anything.

Pablo's waiting lookout for me outside. Within a minute or five, we're back in my suite. I slip the key card back into the wallet, which I left on the writing desk—not smart. Now to return it to the captain who is hopefully happier than when I relieved him of it.

"Okay, stay here. Be right back," I say.

But Mister Cool is out cold on my bed.

DEBRIEF

MINDY

At ten the next morning we're shown into a hotel business room. Mom and Sanchia are as hungover as Clem is bored. None of us have slept much. Someone on his team woke us early this morning with a knock that could've broken down a wall and told us to stop texting—for security reasons—or they'd take our phones, and that we'd meet later to discuss "what we found".

We take our places at a table. Pablo and I sit together next to our moms. A technician sits in front of a large monitor showing an FBI screen saver. Special Agent Clem turns out to be pale and six feet tall and he wears his clothes a couple of sizes too large. His tie is pulled down to unbutton the top of his shirt.

"So, you've found something?" Clem sips from a cardboard coffee cup.

I log in, open the Camera app, and hand him my phone, open on the photo of the contents of the wallet.

He puts on his glasses and begins to scroll. "Tell me, where did you get these photographs?" he asks.

"Mindy shot them," Sanchia says.

"Mindy?" he says, pointing at me. "Is that right?" He blinks more and scrolls through the photos again. He adjusts his glasses on his nose. His eyebrows go up. "This one is from his wallet?"

"Yes," I nod.

"We kept that poor man busy at the bar, as you instructed," Mom says, "while Mindy borrowed his wallet. Don't worry; she put it back."

Clem shakes his head and rubs his eyes.

"Excellent work, my dear," Sanchia says to me. "And, Penny, I thought your sweet-talking to the happy captain was . . . inspiring."

"Go to hell," Mom smirks, fiddling with her ear ring.

"Ladies, let's stay on point, shall we?" Clem says, as he pulls his glasses down and looks at them over the rims.

"Did you see the photo we got off his desk?" I ask. "Aren't they papers a captain would have?"

Clem stares at me, his eyes scanning my face. "You said, 'we'?"

"Pablo and I. He was my lookout."

Pablo leans forward on the table. "Sir, the *Jian Mei 5* supplied the fish factory."

"That's right. And the components for the pills. That ship is under our control now. They found 4-AP, a substance used to make fentanyl. A chemist on the ship was experimenting with fentanyl formulations on patients. Burials at sea are their preferred method of disposing of the dead, though they'd also thrown a crew hand overboard.

"So, if admissible, these photographs will give us the evidence to tie the *Jian Mei 5* to deliveries of narcotics to the US and Mexico. Cutting off the fentanyl, not only to Long Island, but also to the Mexican cartels, will save thousands of lives. "You two," he says pointing at us, "have been helpful in this case. However, I would advise you to stay away from dangerous situations like this. Things can go very wrong."

"I know, boy, can they ever," Pablo says.

"What do you mean?" Clem asks.

Pablo throws up his palms. "I find a hole in the ground and I end up on a fish factory in the middle of the Atlantic Ocean." But Pablo is not telling the whole story: he made that happen. I know him. He got out exactly when he wanted to. He wanted to help our dads and he did something about it.

"Agent Clem," I say, "sometimes you have to take action, 'cause if you don't, then things can go worse than very wrong."

"That's true. If something looks wrong you have to say something. You can't keep things secret."

I'm getting the impression he's really talking to Mom. She should have acted when she saw Dad sinking. But Pablo and I chased out his secret.

"So, Agent Clem, where does this leave us? Where's my husband?" Mom asks.

He slowly opens the file folder in front of him. "What I can tell you is this: US citizens fleeing the US to foreign registered vessels are not protected by them. We exerted our Special Maritime and Territorial Jurisdiction in order to board. Last night, FBI choppers dropped the Critical Incident Response Group, CIRG, onto the factory ship. Neither your husband nor your son, ma'am," he shoots a glance at Sanchia, "were found. Now we know they evaded us by powerboating to Bermuda. We only apprehended him because of that young man." He points at Pablo. "Your husband is now in custody awaiting deployment to the US."

"Really? More questioning?" Mom asks.

"No. He's under arrest," Clem says.

"My husband didn't evade you; they were escaping that evil

ship. You can't arrest him for that," Mom says. "If you'd shown up sooner, they wouldn't have had to make a run for Bermuda."

"Mrs. MacKay, I'm not going to argue this case with you—and it's not closed. There's still an ongoing investigation into the counterfeit prescription drugs that your husband's sister was trafficking. There's a picture emerging of your sister-in-law, Beth—"

"Yeah, I bet there is—she's an aimless flake who takes advantage of people like my husband," Mom says.

Beth is a creep, but using her as an excuse is not going to work for Mom. I remember Doctor Patel telling us about the detox pills at the hospital. But if they're laced with fentanyl then who can doctors trust when treating addicted patients? And that's okay with Beth…and maybe Dad too?

"What we don't know, Mrs. MacKay," the agent says, "is why this shadow organization would want to kill addicts who've been paying them millions in repeat business?"

Tears run down Mom's face. "Because," she sniffs, "Lucas wants to get rid of the gangs—just like you do. And he took action, as Mindy said. If their drug gang customers die so does their business. He hoped they'd leave and find other communities."

"So, take their poison somewhere else? Just as long as it's not in your neighborhood. Is that it?" Clem asks.

Mom looks down at her hands and nods.

Sanchia is speechless. But I have been expecting this. I remember Mom crying in her sewing room. She knew this day would come. Finally, she would have to say it's all over for dad. Then what good would her pretty house be? All her do-good work at the Op Shop had suddenly become meaningless. She could stop pretending.

LATER THAT DAY, WE'RE TOLD WE'RE BOOKED ON A FLIGHT BACK to JFK. I'm standing at the airport windows overlooking the airstrip watching the airliners come and go when I notice a panel van driving to a smaller twin-engine plane. Uniformed law enforcement officers get out and open the back.

"Mom," I call, "take a look at this."

She comes over.

"Could this be—"

But her guess is cut short by the sight of Dad being helped out of the van and walked toward the plane.

She is sobbing as she watches her handcuffed husband in chained ankles being led to the plane. I shift closer to Mom and put my arm over her shoulder. She hugs me hard, shaking. "Oh, Min. I am so sorry. I have been a terrible mother. I have kept this secret from you for so long. I always hoped it would pass and we could go on with our lives."

But I can't bring myself to tell her that I knew this day would come. I should say I'm sorry too. Instead, I say, "It'll be all right. Now it *has* passed. We can stop lying to each other."

She nods and wipes a tear off her cheek. She looks at me with exhausted, bloodshot eyes. "Yes. Oh, thank you for giving me another chance, Mindy, my precious heart."

I smooth her hair, just like she does to me.

EPILOGUE

MINDY

A FEW MONTHS HAVE PASSED SINCE BERMUDA AND THE END OF OUR world as we knew it. It seems like years. But on this particular November afternoon, the Sunday after Thanksgiving, with a chill creeping down the slope we've bundled up for our walk to the top of the rise. Candy has made it to the top, dragging Peter all the way. At her fascinating telephone pole, Peter stops to wipe his brow; he pants harder than Candy as he looks out over the sound.

"Does he still do this walk every morning?" I ask Pablo.

"I see them go out," he says, "but maybe not to the top every time. It's been a big change for him . . . but he's been great."

"Peter knows all about change."

"It's true. He always listens for it," Pablo says.

"I finally get it. It's not just what he can hear, it's what's behind the sound—I should know—the hum, the vibration, the hiss from some restless object that leads to what's causing it. That's why people don't change—they don't want to know what's underneath."

Pablo has been staring at his feet, listening to my theory about listening, and then he proves he's heard me as well. "And, as all that nasty stuff invaded your mind you listened because that restless object was your dad," he says. "And the sound that object made was darkness. He didn't care. Peter once told me that caring is a hand inside a glove of light."

Peter's wisdom. I watch our old mentor stare out at the sound with a smile as wide as the sound.

"Mindy!" He calls out to me. He licks his finger and holds it into the facing breeze. Fred, Sanchia and Mom are trying to figure out what he's doing. But Pablo and I know.

"Yes, I remember, Peter," I call back. "Now I'm a zephyr, blowing in from New York City on the west wind."

"Really, you guys," Sanchia says. "With your codes and signals and funny words. What are you planning? And please let me and Penny in on your secrets before you go off to defend someone's struggle."

Are our own struggles ever over?

"Or," Mom says, "at least give us a heads-up, so we can stay at the Ritz next time?"

Sanchia high-fives her.

"Come," Fred says. "I've made paella. It's sangria time."

Pablo and I amble down the slope next to each other, lost in our memories of that fateful weekend. We pass Peter and Fred's boarded-up farm stand, which must have been inviting in a countrified way over the summer.

"Peter said we had a bumper crop of sunflowers," Pablo says.

"Of course. With Sanchia's social marketing and Fred's new shingles and roof and your signs, I bet it sold every sunflower."

Pablo hesitates and faces me. "Do you miss him?" he asks.

"My dad? Sure, but at least he's alive. And it won't be a life sentence. He'll get out one day. And, I can tell you this," I say, waving my finger at him, "Dad will never...oh, never mind."

How can I say he'll never get addicted again? Though, perhaps years of being sober in prison will help him recover and give him a second chance.

"In the meantime, you've started running," Pablo, the optimist says.

I pull my shoulders back and give him a thumbs up. "Seems I'm a better runner than a soccer player. There are races every week in Central Park. You should visit. Come for New Year's Eve. We'll do the midnight run in the park. And afterwards, we'll warm up with Mom's bitter coffee and pannettone bread pudding."

"Wow. I'm there," he says. "So, you're enjoying it?"

"We like the city. When Dad fell to pieces, Mom and I grew closer in a way I never imagined. Over time I'm realizing I'm more like her than I thought."

"Maybe, except you're smarter."

He makes me smile. "I don't know about that."

"I do. If you hadn't suggested my dad work with that detective things could have gone bad quickly," he says, turning his face into the wind to blow his hair out of his eyes. "And if you hadn't made your dad drop me at Peter's place, we wouldn't be living with him right now. You gave us a better life."

"Your family gave *him* a life again," I say. "Thank you for what you did—cutting off the drugs. That's what drove the gangs out."

"Yeah, for now. Maybe."

"Yes, maybe. What do you want, perfection? You tried. You helped. You put your life on the line."

"I did that for you. But I also did that for *my* dad, for our family, so we could stay in the US. I was just looking after myself. And, I didn't want to lose you as a friend."

But he'll never admit he did so much more than just keep a friend; he did something extraordinary.

"Pablo, I will always be your friend, even when you are great —and you will be at art school," I say. I nudge a little closer, and something makes me take hold of his hand with both of mine. Our eyes connect. "No matter what happens to you, I will always care about you because you cared about me. You looked after me."

"And you believed in me—I have always known that," he says, squeezing my hand. "You never gave up on me."

"And I never will. Your mom's sacred hope has rubbed off on you and it inspires me. You always push me to be better than I think I can be, to be bold, look farther ahead—like we're already twenty. There are no half-measures with you, no partial fixes— you're all in, whatever you do. As we get older Pablo, I will cherish you more and more—never less."

$\backsim$

JOIN MY READER GROUP

I look forward to an ongoing conversation with readers like you, and think of my newsletter emails as conversation starters. I am interested in your feedback regarding the challenge I set for myself: to expose the truth of the story to you, the reader. When I get a perspective that I had not considered previously I am enormously grateful.

Regardless of what facets and flaws the truth might unearth, I strive to keep my writing intellectually curious and emotionally honest, even if the dramatic truth lurks in the dark waters of the story's subtext. This goal for me is as fundamental as the affirmation of life.

Because these wide-ranging concepts cannot be fully explored within the constraints of a story, I invite you to join me as I extend the conversation in my newsletters.

Once you sign up, you will have exclusive access to materials that are not available elsewhere, such as essays, drafts (I am always looking for beta readers), and early ideas that will eventually end up in my published books.

I want to hear your ideas, your comments and thoughts. Join my newsletter here:

https://geoffreywellsfiction.com/signup-to-my-newsletter/

BIBLIOGRAPHY

THE TRILOGY FOR FREEDOM

The Ice Wine Books of Geoffrey Wells

Book One:
A Fado for the River
A thriller about a quest for personal freedom in a nation struggling for its liberation.
Book Two:
Atone for the Ivory Cloud
A thriller about identity and conservation—and those who exploit both.
Book Three:
The Drowning Bay
An eco-thriller about finding belonging in a lost ecosystem. Two women protecting a bay . . . their way.

Please visit my website:

https://geoffreywellsfiction.com/

ALSO PUBLISHED BY GEOFFREY
WELLS:

MOONGLOW

A children's book written by Peggy Dickerson and Illustrated by Cynthia Wells

~.~

The pages in Moonglow take the young reader into an eastern North America forest. Realistic animals are caught in the moonbeams as birds, deer, fireflies, frogs, and water striders magically play among indigenous plants. A factual appendix at the back of the book invites the young reader to learn more about the woodland creatures as well as interesting facts about the moon. This teaching aid is filled with vocabulary, science, and creative writing lessons.

https://moonglowkids.com/

BOOK DISCUSSION

QUESTIONS FOR THE CURIOUS READER.

Mom's been looking after Dad so we can continue to live in our beautiful, lonely house.

==> Why does Mindy call her house lonely?

It's clear to me now that the job she had for me at the Op Shop was to make her feel like she had a daughter who loved her. But she forgot to give me that job.

==> Why does Mindy think her mom forgot to give her the job of loving her?

Team Cruz will know what to do—our team motto is Everyone for Himself—provided Mom knows. So now, as always, I will include her using our special method.

==>How is the Cruz team motto actually part of Pablo's safety net?

An ambulance siren wails in the night. But with Peter's, Mindy's and my one-hundred-and-four years of experience we can solve these problems. The ambulance I heard rushes past us, sowing its frantic lights like seeds of hope.

==>What is the difference between ordinary hope and sacred hope in this story?

Mom and Sanchia look lovely, so in control, as if somehow each is the salve for the other's emptiness—the missing son, the missing husband. And for this I love them both.

==>Why does Mindy love them more, now that she's seen them like this?

ACKNOWLEDGMENTS

With this book I continue my authorpreneur path, depending on people to deliver the highest possible quality so I can give the reader a satisfying reading experience. Almost without exception, I have encountered collaborators who have generously gone above and beyond what I required. It is these people I want to thank for the outcome of this book.

For the genius design and illustration of the cover I want to thank Leah Palmer Preiss for her countless design and illustration ideas that visually inform a mystery about drug smugglers and addiction. Brilliant work, Leah. Brilliant!

I am extremely grateful to my Beta Reading Group for their patience with being asked to read draft after draft. Their feedback has been extremely helpful to me pointing out things that simply did not occur to me. I particularly want to thank Peggy Dickerson (the author of *Moonglow*, which I published), for her comments based on a thirty-year teaching career. In addition, I would be remiss if I didn't thank best-selling author Pamela Burford, for her guidance on point of view and first-person narrative.

I would like to thank licensed therapist and drug and alcohol counselor, Lindsay Larris for her close read of the pharmaceutical aspects of the story, assuring the reader that the drugs are correctly referenced, while of course, allowing my fictional use of them to run riot.

I want to thank my exceptional editorial team: To Britta Jensen for pushing me to take hard decisions in the development editing, to Jules Hucke, who's exacting copy editing made my book shine and to Laura Edge for her expert proofreading.

Finally, I want to thank Susi and Chris Young for giving me access to Peter Young's navy records. He inspired the creation of Peter, Pablo and Mindy's mentor.

With this book once again, I thank Cynthia, my wife for her patience and unwavering encouragement throughout the entire process of bringing it into the world—from idea to launch day and beyond.

AN ICE WINE BOOK

Published by
Ice Wine Productions, Inc.
P.O. 261, Peconic, NY 11958
www.geoffreywellsfiction.com

Never Less

We all need a safety net, but need a true friend even more...

ISBN 979-8-9863836-1-3 (Print book)
ISBN 979-8-9863836-2-0 (ebook)

Cover design and illustration by Leah Palmer Preiss.

Version 1.0

195

ABOUT GEOFFREY WELLS

The new release by Geoffrey Wells is a middle grade mystery, *Never Less (2022)*. It is a thriller for young readers twelve and up, that will help them deal with the opioid crisis in an adventurous, and relatable way, which will empower them to conquer even the toughest grown-up problems.

Geoffrey Wells is the author of three stand-alone novels on freedom, now a series entitled, *The Trilogy for Freedom.(2021)*

In his latest eco-thriller, *The Drowning Bay (2021)*, based on a water crisis and climate change, Wells looks at what the responsibility of freedom means and how it might lead to finding a belonging in a lost ecosystem.

Inspired by his ascent of Kilimanjaro in 2003 and horrified by the devastation of elephants, he published, *Atone for the Ivory Cloud (2016)*. He explores how tolerance of life grants the freedom to choose.

In *A Fado for the River (2011)*, based on his experience in Mozambique one year before the Portuguese revolution spilled into the colony, Wells explores the quest for personal freedom, which grew out of a nation struggling for its liberation.

Wells started writing fiction after a career in information technology, rising to vice president and chief information officer at two major broadcasting companies.

Concurrent with his corporate life, he wrote and produced an award-winning animated film, *The Shadow of Doubt*, directed by his wife, Cynthia Wells, an animator and painter. The film showed in 27 film festivals and won 5 awards.

In 2015 he edited, designed and published the award-winning children's book, *Moonglow* written by Peggy Dickerson and illustrated by Cynthia Wells.

He lives on the North Fork of Long Island where he participates in triathlons and swims the open water with his wife and their dog, Luciano.

PLEASE GET HELP

A RESOURCE GUIDE

If you or someone you know needs help with opioid addiction please get help right now. Most police departments, pharmacies, harm reduction centers, and even some libraries can provide *free Narcan kits* to prevent possible overdoses. There is treatment, and it is available if loved ones need it.
Here are some of the ways to get Narcan (naloxone) kits.

New York State:
https://www1.nyc.gov/site/doh/health/health-topics/naloxone.page
https://www1.nyc.gov/assets/doh/downloads/pdf/basas/naloxone-list-of-prevention-programs.pdf
https://www1.nyc.gov/assets/doh/downloads/pdf/basas/naloxone-list-of-pharmacy.pdf

USA National Resources:
https://www.samhsa.gov/find-help/national-helpline

https://www.cdc.gov/opioids/overdoseprevention/help-resources.html

https://www.smartrecovery.org/

https://www.addictioncenter.com/treatment/12-step-programs/
narcotics-anonymous/

In addition to the above, the author recommends viewing the
Politics and Prose interview that
Beth Macy (Dopesick) did with Carl Erik Fisher (an addiction
physician and bioethicist).
https://www.youtube.com/watch?v=75uzyhvM5YE

~.~
Medical advice disclaimer.
The information in this book is not intended or implied to be a
substitute for professional medical advice, diagnosis or treatment.
All content in this book, including text, is for *fictional
entertainment purposes only*. Ice Wine Books makes no
representation and assumes no responsibility for the accuracy of
information contained in this book. You are encouraged to confirm
any information in this book with other sources, some of which are
listed above.
NEVER DISREGARD PROFESSIONAL MEDICAL ADVICE
OR DELAY SEEKING MEDICAL TREATMENT
BECAUSE OF SOMETHING YOU HAVE READ IN THIS
BOOK.

DID YOU ENJOY THIS BOOK?

I appreciate you spending your time on my book.
You should know that reviews make a big difference to the success of a book.
I hope the time I spent writing and researching this book meant a great read for you.
Your review can be as short as you like, but honestly, other readers will find your insight helpful, so please share and help them make up their minds about reading the book.
Your review will help this book rank higher, and for that, my career will be most grateful.

Post your review on Goodreads, here:

https://www.goodreads.com/book/show/61836895-never-less

. . . or post your review at the ebook store, or the bookstore where you bought the book.
Stay safe and thank you very much!
Geoffrey.

9 798986 383613